SAMSON OPTION

SHARON GEYER

FaithWalk
PUBLISHING

Grand Haven, Michigan

©2004 Sharon A. Geyer

Published by FaithWalk Publishing
333 Jackson Street, Grand Haven, Michigan 49417

All rights reserved. No part of this book may be reproduced or transmitted in any form by any means, electronic or mechanical, including photocopying and recording, or by any information storage and retrieval system, except as may be expressly permitted by the 1976 Copyright Act or by the publisher. Requests for permission should be made in writing to: FaithWalk Publishing, 333 Jackson Street, Grand Haven, Michigan, 49417

Scripture quotations marked "KJV" are taken from the Holy Bible, King James Version, Cambridge, 1769.

Printed in the United States of America

09 08 07 06 05 04   7 6 5 4 3 2 1

Library of Congress Cataloging-in Publication Data

Geyer, Sharon.
  The Samson option / by Sharon Geyer.
    p. cm.
  ISBN 0-9724196-7-5 (pbk. : alk. paper)
  1. Americans--Israel--Fiction. 2. Islamic sects--Fiction. 3. Jewish women--Fiction. 4. Mahdism--Fiction. 5. Israel--Fiction. 6. Dreams--Fiction. I. Title.
    PS3607.E94S26 2004
    813'.6--dc22
                              2003021430

To Rodwin and Shadwin

Acknowledgments

I wish to thank Joan Oppenheimer, Betty Webb, and Ron Carlson, for teaching me the craft of writing. I also wish to thank my talented and able editor, Louann Werksma.

"...mercy rejoiceth against judgment."
James 3:13 (KJV)

And it came to pass, when their hearts were merry, that they said, Call for Samson, that he may make us sport. And they called for Samson out of the prison house; and he made them sport: and they set him between the pillars.

And Samson said unto the lad that held him by the hand, Suffer me that I may feel the pillars whereupon the house standeth, that I may lean upon them.

Now the house was full of men and women; and all the lords of the Philistines were there; and there were upon the roof about three thousand men and women, that beheld while Samson made sport.

And Samson called unto the LORD, and said, O Lord God, remember me, I pray thee, and strengthen me, I pray thee, only this once, O God, that I may be at once avenged of the Philistines for my two eyes.

And Samson took hold of the two middle pillars upon which the house stood, and on which it was borne up, of the one with his right hand, and of the other with his left.

And Samson said, Let me die with the Philistines. And he bowed himself with all his might; and the house fell upon the lords, and upon all the people that were therein. So the dead which he slew at his death were more than they which he slew in his life.
Judges 16: 25–30 (KJV)

Chapter 1

Samuel Rosen passed from this life into the next with no struggle, no anxiety as the thin blade severed the artery in his throat.

His killer calmly stepped back out of range of the spurting blood, wiped off his knife with a corner of the duvet, and whispered *Allah akbar*, God is great.

Simultaneously, the second assassin looked into Dr. Klein's empty bedroom and mumbled *pedar sag*, labeling the missing doctor the offspring of a dog. Turning quickly, he left the bedroom and joined his partner in the hallway. "She's not in her bed, check the bathroom," he said with urgency.

Together, they approached the bathroom off the hallway and, detecting no light under the closed door, gently pushed it open. A quick sweep of a flashlight revealed no one there. Calmly and methodically they searched every room in Bet Shalom, including the empty bedrooms of the patients, who had gone home for the Passover.

The intruders, dressed in black hoods and leather boots, moved with practiced assurance. They paused to get their bearings, checking the sounds: ticking clock, ancient pipes gurgling, and sighing in the walls.

They knew the layout of Bet Shalom, a private mental clinic, also called the House of Peace. Their targets should have been sleeping in their beds. Like goats before the slaughter at the Feast of Sacrifice, they would not know when their throats were slit.

"Check her bedroom again. And the balcony," whispered the taller man.

They retraced their steps down the hall, then froze at the sound of a key turning in the outside door of the kitchen. They moved silently to meet the unsuspecting doctor as she came in from the garden.

"She will die in the kitchen instead of peacefully in her bed," whispered the shorter of the two.

A woman's hand reached for the light switch. Before she could scream, a gloved hand clamped over her mouth and another hand slit her throat with a stiletto.

In the quiet thrill of bloodlust, the assassins slipped out the kitchen door, buried their weapons under a fir tree, and returned to the rental car parked near the Holocaust Museum. They disappeared into the fog like wraiths.

By seven a.m. they stood by their packed baggage in the lobby of Jerusalem's American Colony Hotel with the rest of their tour group, but the mini-vans transporting them to the airport were thirty minutes late. In fluent Italian, the assassins grumbled with the others about Israeli laxness. With their dark hair and olive complexions, they looked no different from the other pilgrims. At Ben Gurion Airport they were delayed for a security check of their luggage. Then, boarding the buses taking them to the jet, they waited while a security man made a head count. They felt composed and triumphant, looking forward to their next assignment.

Heftsibah Klein stood on her bedroom balcony smoking her last pack of imported French cigarettes. After shoving the last stub into a potted geranium, she made her way to the kitchen where the cook kept cheap Israeli cigarettes. She found a half empty pack of *Time* and smiled.

"The kind Ari smoked," she said aloud, fondly remembering the young soldier who had been her patient the previous year. She wondered where Ari Ben Chaim was having his first smoke this gloomy morning. She slipped the rumpled packet into the pocket of her robe, and took a book of matches off the gas stove, promising herself to give up smoking due to her history of hypertension.

She felt a slight breeze and saw that the back door wasn't fully closed. She screamed when she saw the bloody body of the cook crumpled on the kitchen floor.

Moshe loved cows. He'd milked them every morning for the past twenty years and loved everything connected with dairy farming—except for the new emphasis on high production. He believed it harmed his cows, and he tried unsuccessfully to prevent this technology from taking hold on the kibbutz.

Before the sun rose, he rolled out of bed, careful not to wake his wife. He pulled on navy blue dungarees and a matching shirt, then went to boil water and heat milk for coffee. As he always did, he left a glass of hot milky coffee by the bed for Shifra. Stepping out of the small cottage, he reached for the knee-high rubber boots on the open shelf, slipped them on, and headed to the dairy barn before the sun appeared over the Golan Heights.

His thoughts turned to his son Ari, who had been an assistant milker before joining the army. It had been a year since father and son last met. After the army, Ari had gone to India to "find himself." He shook his head sadly and headed to the barn.

The sweet smell of fresh alfalfa mingled with the comforting odor of cow manure greeted him as he shoved open the big door. With the milking done by machines now, he missed the physical contact of hand milking. This was considered progress. He knew the name of all the cows and reassuringly patted each one before he bent down to attach the metal milker. In this position, he did not see the stranger standing in the doorway of the barn.

This stranger was not dressed like a farmer or one of the American volunteers. He wore fine leather boots and a black hood over his head. The visitor sniffed at the unaccustomed smells, then drew a slim dagger out of a sheath strapped to his ankle. Walking almost daintily, trying not to soil his boots, he approached Moshe unseen.

The cows stirred restlessly in their stalls. Two bellowed as if in warning, but Moshe paid no heed. He died instantly, never knowing who murdered him, or why. His blood mingled with the muck and straw to form a viscous mortar. The gentle cows were the only witnesses.

The man in black leather opened the unlocked door and slipped unseen into the cottage. Shifra sat up in bed, reached for the coffee, now just warm enough for her taste, and drank it down to the thick grounds in the bottom of the glass.

Only Jews would drink coffee diluted with milk. The hooded man in the shadows looked on with disgust, an expression that quickly changed to the bland aspect of the professional doing his job. His timing was off by one minute, so his target would not die in her sleep as planned.

Sensing, rather than hearing, the presence of an intruder, Shifra swung her bare feet out of bed. Before her toes touched the floor the stiletto found its target. She blinked as to confirm that her worst fears had come true.

He preferred not to see the horror in his victims' eyes before he cut their throats, unless the killing was for revenge. But he harbored no animosity towards this middle-aged Jewess who had raised the Holy One, the hidden *Mahdi*. He never questioned his orders to eliminate these infidels who had been intimately acquainted with the Twelfth and last Imam.

Those close to Ari Ben Chaim must die. This curious twist of providence that decreed the Mahdi would be succored in the midst of his enemies seemed entirely plausible to the assassin. The deaths of Moshe and Shifra also appeared reasonable. They were despised Israelis.

He left Ari's mother lying on a blood-soaked pillow, her glazed eyes wide open. Without encountering another soul, he hurried to the United Nations jeep hidden in the wadi below the kibbutz. There he pulled off the black garments to reveal a United Nations peace-keeper's uniform. He grinned, remembering how easily he had bribed the Pakistani officer stationed on the border between Israel and Syria. He drove east, crossing the Jordan River where it joined the Sea of Galilee. Ascending the Golan Heights, he drove beyond the settlement town of Qatzrin before he encountered an Israeli Army roadblock. Imitating the clipped diction of a Pakistani, he showed his United Nations papers to a soldier who waved him on with a disdainful shrug.

Twenty minutes later he drove into the no-man's-land that separated Israel from Syria. Ahead he saw the deserted village of Qunetra that served as the United Nations observation post. His bribed accomplice was on duty, and they exchanged vehicles.

By the time a hysterical volunteer found the body of Moshe and ran to tell Shifra, the assassin was well on his way to Damascus.

The train pulled out of London's Victoria station and picked up speed as it rushed past the suburbs. A young man with a black mustache, carrying an umbrella and the *London Times* neatly strapped to his battered suitcase, chose a window seat. Rain fell in sheets against the window, obscuring his view. He unstrapped the *Times*, folded it precisely in quarters, and proceeded to read.

Passengers departed and boarded as the train continued north to Harrogate. At noon the man got up, went to the dining car, and ordered lamb chops and a baked potato. He sent a cup of weak, milky coffee back to the kitchen, ordering another, strong and black. He left a tip sufficient to satisfy the waiter but not one to remark about at the end of his shift.

At the train station in Harrogate, he hired a taxi to take him to a moderately priced hotel known for its therapeutic spa. In the privacy of his room, he opened his suitcase and spread his tools on the bedcover.

First he unwrapped a stiletto in its ankle strap. Then he caressed the twelve-millimeter handgun with a silencer. Cautiously, he picked up the walking stick that concealed a poison tip. He had prepared for several approaches to his target. There was little possibility of gaining access to a British spinster's flat without being seen. His partners in Israel might break into a mental clinic at night or boldly walk into a kibbutz. In England, the Brotherhood handled assignments differently. He prided himself on his ability to understand the British mentality.

The assassin's father had sent him to boarding school in London. Now his accent was flawlessly upper middle class. He felt more comfortable in the urban sophistication of London than his birthplace, but he never forgot he was a *Seyyed*, direct descendant of the Prophet. Like his father, he held the British in contempt. On his first assignment for the followers of the

Mahdi, there must be no mistakes.

He'd sufficiently established Miss Queller's routine after two weeks of surveillance. A retired nurse, she slept late and never breakfasted outside her home. Monday through Friday, she emerged from her flat on the ground floor and walked to the nearest Boots pharmacy or spent an hour shopping in Marks and Spencers.

At precisely one o'clock each afternoon, she ate lunch in the same tea shop. Occasionally a woman friend, similarly gray and stout, joined her. The only difference in outward appearance between his target and her friend was Miss Queller's penchant for sturdy walking shoes. The other woman wore stylish high-heeled shoes.

He attributed that difference in style to the years Miss Queller had lived in the Middle East. She had been the nurse in charge of the orphanage in Jerusalem. Why had she taken a personal interest in little Ari? She would now pay with her life.

On Saturday, the woman left the flat to shop at the butcher and the fresh produce shop near her home. She never missed the eleven a.m. service at St. Paul's on Sunday, returned home, and did not leave her flat again. She had no social life and never went out in the evenings.

Typically English, the assassin concluded.

He sat at the small round table near the window where he could see when she entered. The fragrance of fresh bread coming from the kitchen reminded him of his childhood in the mountains above Tehran. Before each meal, his mother had dispatched a servant to buy flat loaves fresh from the bakery. The servant always favored him with the first piece of warm nan.

The tea room door opened with a swish of cold air that jolted him out of his reverie. Involuntarily, he sat a little straighter as Miss Queller placed her mackintosh on the rack by the door and left her dripping umbrella against the wall, then took her regular seat in front of the window and ordered. She ate her tomato sandwich while watching the flow of pedestrians outside. Presently, the waitress brought her a second pot of tea along with a cream cake. The tea room was now full.

He sat close enough to Miss Queller to observe the tiny spot of cream on her upper lip. In the unflattering light of the window, he could see deep lines on her face. The middle eastern sun did that to the complexion of the fair-skinned British. His mother, about the same age as Miss Queller, had a face still plump and smooth.

He compared his mother and his victim without moral dilemma because they did not exist in the same universe. Everything outside of Iran existed in a different frame of reference. He knew the British seldom recognized and never acknowledged this point of view.

Finishing his cup of coffee, he put a pound note on the table. Then he rose awkwardly from his seat, like a man who has wrenched his back gardening or playing tennis. He placed his right hand on the cane and put his thumb on the rounded handle. Turning to his right he maneuvered the tip of the cane toward the spinster's lower back, smoothly inserting the lethal tip into her spinal cord.

Immediate paralysis set in. Miss Queller's vocal cords would not obey her frantic mental command to cry out in pain. Her frightened eyes stared woodenly ahead.

Chapter 2

Ari stood in front of a desk in the Israeli Consulate in Bombay. He wiped his neck with a sweat stained rag. The motion from the overhead fan moved the moist heat around the narrow room in slow waves.

"My condolences," said the clerk behind the desk as he handed Ari a folded telegram.

Ari reluctantly read the contents of the message from his kibbutz. With growing dread he learned that his parents, Shifra and Moshe Ben Chaim, had died ten days earlier and the burial had already taken place. Both? The same day? He looked mutely at the clerk.

Various scenarios tumbled through his mind. Katushka rockets fired from Lebanon? A road accident in the kibbutz-owned jeep? A bomb placed by local Palestinians? All three disasters were daily possibilities in his homeland. His throat felt unbearably dry when he tried to speak.

His fellow countryman understood, filled a paper cup at the water cooler, and handed it to him.

"Can I help you make plane reservations?"

Ari mumbled "No," then hurried out the door before his tears could betray him. Like a man sleepwalking, he joined the heavy stream of Bombay's pedestrians, carts, and bicycles. Approaching the shoreline of the Indian Ocean, the traffic thinned as people continued to the right or left. Nobody paid attention to the tall young man with tears streaming down his cheeks.

Ari headed across the sandy beach toward the water's edge. Staring at the expanse of blue-green water, he slipped off his leather sandals and walked barefoot in the cool sand where the dirty froth lapped at the shore.

His head ached, and he closed his eyes against the glare of the sun. The smell of rotten fish and overly ripe coconuts mingled in his nostrils, reminding him of his alien status in this exotic land, so far from the scent of Galilee roses, the pungent aroma of his mother's lemon cake.

He walked over to a clump of coconut trees and reread the telegram. It was brief and to the point. His parents, Shifra and Moshe, had died the same day and were buried together. He should return as soon as possible.

This was not the first time he was orphaned in one day. Ari's thoughts slipped back to his eighteenth birthday, the day his adopted father showed him the records. His birth mother had wrapped him in a clean white scarf and placed him in a dumpster during the Six Day War, just after the Israeli Army captured the Temple Mount.

A soldier heard his cries and took him to the Women's International Zionist Organization orphanage in Bet Hakarem. There a nurse named the baby boy Ari because of the lion-shaped birthmark on his cheek.

Now, sitting in the sand of a sticky Bombay beach, Ari felt abandoned again, this time by his adopted parents. He watched the tide creep higher, soaking his trousers. His body sagged and he felt overwhelmed with grief. The rays of the setting sun struck his face as he softly fingered the delicate birthmark on his cheek, an unconscious gesture he always made under stress.

In the sudden onset of night, as if a celestial hand had pulled down the shades, his thoughts turned to Lily, the American woman who had become his friend and confidant at Bet Shalom. No, he thought, she had become more than a friend. He liked her lopsided smile, and when tears had welled in her eyes when he announced his trip to India, he knew he loved her.

It hurt to think about her now. Why had he felt the need to get away from Jerusalem? And Lily? He had never felt so close to anyone. She might be crazy with her talk about archangels, but many considered him crazy, too. What soldier in his right mind would hand his rifle to his commanding officer and walk away?

His parents couldn't understand his actions, and he regretted the shame he had caused them.

Lily thought his actions made sense under the circumstances. "I wish every soldier in the Israeli Army could do the same," she had said. "Israel can't surrender to the enemy, but I respect your stand of nonviolence."

Ari stood and straightened his shoulders to shake off the burden of self pity. *I must go home to pay respects to my parents' memory. Then I'll ask Lily to marry me.*

Encouraged by the thoughts of a future with Lily, Ari made his way back to the city to book his ticket home.

A bearded man wearing a green turban and a dirty tunic watched Ari collect his ticket and board the plane. A bribe to the Lufthansa employee produced Ari's itinerary: Bahrain–Frankfurt–Tel Aviv.

Five minutes after the plane left the tarmac the man sent a telegram to the Iranian Embassy in Damascus. The telegram was addressed to Reza Ali Najmabadi, a minor clerk in the economic trade office. Reza facilitated the mountain of paperwork produced by the weekly shipments of missiles from Iran to Syria.

The weaponry were state of the art but the Iranians operated without computers, using hand-copied requisitions.

"My mother's brother in Calcutta is asking for more money." Reza feigned indignation before his colleagues. "What can I do? He has nine children, six of them girls."

He tucked the telegram into the breast pocket of his white shirt until he could decode it in the privacy of his apartment.

All the employees in the Iranian foreign service sent half their pay to relatives back home. Under Khomeini, the economy was growing, but it took time for improvements to reach the general population. Everyone in the office nodded or smiled in commiseration with Reza's plight.

After Reza decoded Ari's flight number and time of arrival at Ben Gurion airport, he sent a coded message to Jamal, a Druze living on the Israeli side of the Golan Heights.

Jamal was a friend and sympathizer of the Brotherhood, though not a member. His family had arrived on the Golan two hundred years before. His father served twenty-one years in the British Army and was later given the Arabic honorific "Bek" by Jordan's King Abdullah. After the Six Day War when Israel conquered the West Bank, Jamal switched sides and became a tracker for the Israeli Army until he miscalculated and stepped on a land mine.

As a Druze, Jamal shared a doctrine in common with the Mahdi sect, taqiyya, meaning prudence, a word borrowed from the Koran. Jamal, like the Shi'ites, felt obliged by conscience to hide his intimate feelings and especially his religious convictions among the enemies of the faith.

This law of secrecy, which maintains and legalizes lying, enabled Jamal to work for the Israeli Army with no pangs of conscience. It also enabled him to pretend to identify with the Iranians. They needed him to smuggle an Israeli into Syria. No problem.

Alive or dead? Jamal signaled back. When he learned the soldier would be alive and must be treated with care, he almost backed off.

In the end, Jamal put aside his reservations and agreed to deliver the soldier at the prearranged place. Time would reveal the Brotherhood's motives. There was no need to give away his personal feelings on the matter, now or ever.

Chapter 3

The doors opened on the far side of the Tel Aviv airport arrival hall. Lily was there to welcome Ari home. She wore her favorite maxi-skirt of soft paisley and a well worn pair of sandals. She never wore makeup, but for this occasion she had dabbed *Anais Anais* on her wrists and throat. Passengers trickled in, searching for their baggage. Then she spotted him, taking note of his new beard, his dark curly hair looking wild and unruly. He wore leather thongs on his feet and carried a canvas duffel bag. Bypassing the luggage carousel he headed for the passport control desk.

Lily saw the female clerk smile, as if she too thought he looked sexy. The clerk punched his identity number into the computer, stamped his passport, and handed it back to him.

When Ari looked over to the glassed partition, Lily's hazel eyes widened with excitement and she waved to him. He smiled at her and mouthed the word shalom and pointed to the men's room door.

Her heart pounding with anticipation, Lily pushed her way out of the crowd. Once outside, she positioned herself along the guard rail so she could watch the exit. If he hadn't stopped in the men's room, she reasoned, he would have been the first person out on the sidewalk. She took a deep breath and closed her eyes as the scent of orange blossoms filled her lungs from the nearby groves.

A Hasidic family emerged first, the father wearing a black coat and fur hat, pushing a baby carriage piled high with packages. Then came the mother holding the hand of a toddler in each of hers.

A middle-aged man with a miniature schnauzer on a leash rushed the dog to the curb for a long pee. This amused Lily. She knew she would never see such a scene in an American airport. Passengers burst out of the double doors in a stream that flowed in proportion to the number and size of their suitcases.

Lily knew that customs officials waved some passengers through. Others had to open every suitcase and carton. But Ari had no luggage and carried only a small duffel bag. He would be out soon, she thought with mounting anticipation. She had missed him more than she was willing to admit to herself until this moment.

The crowds thinned as the newly arrived were kissed, hugged, and directed into waiting vehicles. Lily waited patiently, but still Ari didn't emerge. After twenty minutes, she walked inside to page him. Panic tightened her throat when he didn't acknowledge the page. She rushed outside again to see if he had emerged while she was paging him. Nothing. She asked the first driver waiting in the taxi queue if he had seen someone matching Ari's description. He lifted his chin to indicate a negative.

Inside the terminal again, she sat on a chair wondering what to do next. Then she noticed a man checking the trash bins. He wore the loose fitting jacket that *Shin Bet*, internal security agents, wear to hide their weapons. *Maybe he can help.*

She told him breathlessly, "My friend arrived half an hour ago. He saw me and waved, then he went into the men's room in the arrival hall. Now he's disappeared." Her voice trembled on the last word.

The security man shouted into his radio for someone to check the men's room. Within three minutes he received a reply.

"Come with me," he ordered Lily. He propelled her into a private office.

"Sit," the man said in the abrupt Israeli manner, then turned and left the room.

The room stank of stale cigarettes. Lily wrinkled her nose in disgust. The minutes dragged and her flush of hope began to fade. She nervously chewed her thumbnail. All her romantic expectations, kissing Ari full on the mouth and being hugged and kissed in return, turned into raw panic. At last the door opened and the security man entered alone.

"Where's my friend?" Lily asked. The high pitch of her voice betrayed her growing fear.

"We found no one. There are signs of a struggle. A soap dispenser is broken, the mirror is cracked, and the trash bin overturned. Your friend put up a fight."

"I don't understand." Lily's voice broke. "What happened? How could he just disappear?"

"Drugged and carried out in a utility cart, most likely."

"Without being seen?"

"Not if his attackers were dressed as janitors. I need all the particulars. Your friend's full name?"

"Ari Ben Chaim." Just saying his name caused her tears to flow unheeded.

"Age?"

"Early twenties." She sniffed apologetically, feeling like a wimpy American. A sabra wouldn't cry.

"Address?"

"Kibbutz Shoshanat Ha Emekim ."

"Where was he coming from?"

"Bombay."

The Shin Bet officer nodded knowingly. It was common for recently demobilized soldiers to take off for the Far East.

A second man joined them. Then the passport control clerk was brought in to confirm that Ari did indeed exist.

All flights were held, and the exit to the airport closed. The army set up roadblocks within a ten-mile radius of the airport.

Their swift reaction did not surprise Lily. If terrorists had infiltrated the airport there could be more hiding elsewhere.

She shuddered as she recalled the news reports of the massacre in the coastal town of Nahariyah. PLO commandos had landed on a beach near the town. They burst into an apartment building, kicked open doors, and murdered the startled residents. On the second floor, the occupants heard the shooting and had time to react. A father hid in the closet with his five-year-old daughter. The mother grabbed the baby and hid in the bathtub. The terrorists found the father and daughter, dragged them out to the beach, and clubbed them to death with the butt of their rifles.

Lily shook her head as if to empty it of these horrific images. She bit her lip in frustration, then wiped her eyes on her sleeve.

Ari's sudden disappearance confirmed what she knew, but had been reluctant to acknowledge. She loved him. Memories of the first time they met tumbled into her head in welcome relief against the stark reality of the present.

She had been Dr. Rosen's patient at Bet Shalom for more than a month when she heard the other patients talking about the soldier who refused to carry a weapon. He was now a fellow patient.

Lily was fascinated by Ari from the moment she found him sitting in the library, hunched over a book, compulsively smoking one cigarette after another. At first, all she could see was his mass of black, curly hair.

She sat down on the other end of the couch and waited for him to look up and acknowledge her presence. He kept reading while she studied his face. The heavy eyebrows matched the strong nose. The pale shadows over and above his eyes looked like delicate bruises. His lips were full but finely outlined.

She knew considerable details of his life because the local news had played the story of the Abu Tur incident for days. She decided his picture on the television screen did not do him justice.

Lily coughed, then asked, "What are you reading?"

Ari closed the book and laid it on the sofa. "Shulamit Hareven's book about a *mashuganah*, a crazy woman in Jerusalem." His eyes held a glint of irony.

"I'm not familiar with that author, but the subject matter should interest both of us. I mean, considering where we're presently staying," Lily retorted.

Ari laughed, but she sensed he was not laughing at her.

"Nu? So why are you here?" he asked, still smiling.

"I'm not crazy, if that's what you're thinking."

"Neither am I. What's your story?"

Something in his demeanor inspired Lily's confidence. Maybe it was the contradiction in those wounded eyes. In any event, prudence was not her strong point. Without a pause for reflection, she began.

"I talk with the archangel Michael." She looked up, waiting for a reaction. Taking his silence for approval, she continued. "I was stupid enough to tell this to the immigration clerk when I first arrived in Israel. Next thing I know I'm at Bet Shalom telling my life story to Dr. Rosen. He knows I'm not making it up."

Ari smiled broadly. "Tell me more."

The voice on the airport loudspeaker jolted Lily out of her reverie. "What is she saying? My Hebrew isn't that good."

The man in the next chair replied wearily, "We can leave the terminal now."

Chapter 4

Ari regained consciousness in the cramped trunk of a speeding car. Someone had bound his arms and ankles, and duct tape covered his mouth. The smell of gasoline and exhaust fumes nauseated him. He concentrated on breathing slowly so he wouldn't choke on his own vomit.

Despite the noise of the engine he heard voices from the interior of the vehicle, two men speaking Arabic. Ari strained to hear what they were saying but failed.

The last thing he remembered was waving to Lily before heading to the men's room. *She's still waiting for me at the airport.* His heart sank as he thought of all the things he wanted to say to her. As the minutes passed and he had time to assess his situation, he recalled other Israeli soldiers kidnapped in recent years. The PLO murdered them all, even disemboweling one before tossing his body on the side of the road. Waves of nausea swept over him. Would he meet a similar death?

Ari racked his brain for a plausible reason for his kidnapping. His captors might be Kashmir nationalists from northern India. The consulate in Bombay had warned Israeli tourists to avoid that area after several young men disappeared on a trip to Kashmir. But still, he couldn't believe those nationalists had operatives in Tel Aviv. The more he considered it, the more it seemed probable that the PLO had kidnapped him in retaliation for the Abu Tur incident.

The car traveled for more than an hour at high speed. This told Ari that they were still on the highway. Eventually, the speed slackened and the car idled at what he thought must be a red light. Then the engine accelerated as they climbed a steep hill. By this, Ari guessed that they had reached Haifa and were heading up Mount Carmel.

After twenty minutes, they slowed and came to a total stop. Ari heard the two men get out of the vehicle. The trunk lid opened with a swish of cool, fresh air that Ari breathed in with relief. Hands reached in and jerked him out of the trunk and set him precariously on his feet. He leaned against the car to maintain his balance. In the twilight Ari thought he could detect the outline of houses through the dark shadows.

The bright blaze of approaching headlights swept across the three men, causing Ari's heart to beat faster. Hope of rescue faded when a paneled van stopped and the driver, wearing the white turban of the Druze, got out of the vehicle. The two kidnappers and the truck driver talked out of Ari's hearing, then the Druze walked over and tore the tape off his face. The man put his lit cigarette in Ari's mouth before he could react.

Ari inhaled deeply and said, "The last smoke of the condemned?"

The Druze only grunted and motioned to the others. Ari could do nothing as they picked him up and deposited him, like a sack of rice, into a hidden compartment in the floor of the van.

Later, he heard the crashing of the waves on the ragged cliffs below and knew they were at Rosh HaNikra, the border with Lebanon. He felt a surge of optimism despite the cramped conditions. If they wanted to murder him, they would have done it hours ago. He couldn't figure out why they were taking him to Lebanon, but it meant a chance for him to live, and hope surged in his heart.

The Druze, who had a pass to cross the border, drove all the way to Ba'albek with the throttle wide open. He careened around dangerous mountain curves and overtook vehicles when there was no visible passing lane. His right foot never left the accelerator and his left hand lay heavy on the horn. Obviously, his orders were to get this man to Damascus as soon as possible. The first order of business was to get beyond the demilitarized zone, where the Israeli Army patrolled alongside the South Lebanese Army, and bring his prisoner out of the coffin-like hiding space.

The Druze turned down a narrow dirt track, then parked before a square, one-story dwelling. He extricated Ari and removed his bindings.

Dazed, Ari asked, "Where am I?"

Jamal ignored his question and turned to greet an old man with a face more cunning than pleasant. He wore a long mantle of dark blue cloth embroidered in black. He had tucked a pale blue handkerchief into the folds of the white turban that encircled his tarbush. After receiving a stiff kiss on each cheek from Jamal, the old man ushered them into his home.

"You are most welcome."

Ari thought the greeting certainly excluded himself, but he sat down on the carpet and crossed his legs in imitation of Jamal.

An elderly woman placed bowls of yogurt, cheese, and olives on a white cloth on the carpet, then left the room. Ari reached for the clay water jug and took a long, satisfying drink, then wiped his mouth with the back of his hand.

Jamal offered Ari a cigarette, then changed his mind and gave him the whole pack, with matches.

Ari reluctantly accepted the peace offering. He had encountered Druze during his army service and knew they spoke Hebrew as well as Arabic. They were ethnically derived from Arab stock and their religion was an offshoot of Islam. His captor's government-issue boots signaled that he had been a tracker for the Israeli Army. It meant he was also a sharpshooter, although Ari saw no weapons. With his thirst and hunger satisfied, Ari now thought only of escape.

As if Jamal were prescient, he opened his loose fitting shirt to reveal a dagger tucked into the waist of his pajama-like trousers. He calmly removed the sharp knife and scraped his fingernails.

"I wouldn't try to escape," he said. "You're safe with me, but I can't vouch for anybody else. As soon as it's dark, we go to Damascus. You don't have to go back in that crawl hole. Sit up front with me."

Jamal walked over to a small trunk in one corner of the room. He took out a pair of white baggy trousers and a linen tunic and turban similar to the one he wore. From the bottom of the trunk, he took a small paper packet that held forged identity papers. "You see, all has been arranged by your benefactors."

"Benefactors? You mean kidnappers," Ari said in a burst of anger that he had meant to conceal. He sensed Jamal held no personal animosity towards him but was only performing a job. Ari intended to exploit this neutrality, but now feared he had compromised his plan.

"Believe me, friend, these people hold you in the highest esteem. Why else would you still be alive? You know what they do to captured Israeli soldiers? Same thing they do to the American devils."

"Yeah," Ari said as he remembered the UPI photo of an

American Marine colonel, his bloated body twisting in the wind at the end of a rope. "You're right. They must have other plans for me, or I would already have been tortured and executed."

The road to Damascus, built on the ruins of the old Roman road, was convoluted and steep. They climbed from the Ba'aka Valley to the heights of Mount Hermon on the Golan plateau, passing convoys of Syrian army trucks that forced them within inches of sheer cliff edges. Ari didn't know what he feared most, the unknown kidnappers awaiting him in Damascus or sudden death in a crushed vehicle at the bottom of a gorge.

Jamal chain-smoked furiously, shook his fist, and honked his horn at vehicles he thought were traveling too slowly.

Ari knew enough of the Druze religion to know they divided themselves into the initiated and uninitiated, and that the initiated abstained from the use of tobacco. "So you are not *akil*, initiated?" Ari asked, not realizing his tactlessness.

Jamal gave him a sharp look and replied, "What do you think?"

Ari saw his error and tried too late to drop the subject.

"I am initiated, but I learned to smoke in the army and continue to do so when I am with outsiders."

Jamal lit another cigarette. Ari sensed he had offended the man.

They reached higher altitudes where patches of snow were melting on the lower slopes of Mount Hermon. Along the edges of the highway, purple crocus bloomed in the early spring air along with starry white garlic. To the south, the hills rose in unbroken slopes of snow, the frosty summit veiled in mist. Ari knew that the Israeli Army patrolled the western slopes of the Hermon. If he managed to escape his captors in Damascus, he would have to cross the treacherous volcanic beds on the Golan to reach safety.

One hour outside of the capital city, the traffic slowed due to heavy military vehicles and a large contingent of tanks. Ari had been in India over a year and was now out of touch with day-to-day reality at home. He had no way of knowing if a military confrontation was imminent or if this was merely a routine troop maneuver.

"You've been on this road before?" Ari asked .

Jamal stared ahead.

"Is this kind of troop movement usual?" Ari persisted.

"Maybe," replied Jamal. "We'll stop soon."

The landscape on either side of the road looked barren, yet Ari knew the soil was rich and there was water from nearby Mount Hermon.

"This is your home territory, isn't it?" Ari asked.

"When Syria lost the Golan in sixty-seven, Israel forced many of us to relocate," Jamal replied.

"You live on the Israeli side?" Ari asked.

Jamal grunted a reluctant reply that Ari took for either a yes or a no. "We do not acknowledge borders. We have survived many occupations."

Without warning, he turned off the highway onto a dirt road. They drove on in silence until they could see the outlines of a one-story mud brick building in the distance. As they approached the structure, the Druze explained that they were going to an ancient sanctuary, one of the early monuments of that land that dated back to the times before Druze, Turk, or Arab ruled. The monument had been erected to Nabatean gods of rock and hill, *Drusara* and *Allat*.

They parked and went into the sanctuary. Ari saw a sarcophagus covered with shreds of colored rags. He cautiously lifted the rags to reveal a block of stone worn smooth by the touch of human hands. The snow that had drifted in through the door had melted and lay in muddy pools on the floor. The day was cold, with a leaden sky; Ari shuddered with dark apprehension.

"What now?" he asked.

"We wait for the Brotherhood," Jamal replied. "My assignment is over, yours is just beginning."

Chapter 5

Reza drove due west out of Damascus to the prearranged rendezvous with the Mahdi, a man he considered to be *isma*, infallible, with the divine gift of being impeccable. He wiped his damp brow with a soggy handkerchief and prayed he would not offend. His orders were to pay the Druze driver, then bring the Mahdi to the villa of the secret Brotherhood of the Fatimids.

It still troubled Reza that the one designated the Mahdi was an Israeli citizen, raised as a Jew on a communal farm. "How can the Hidden Imam be a Jew?" he had asked.

His superiors had replied, "The Mahdi is none other than the mysterious *Shiloh*, to whom would be transferred, in the latter days, the spiritual authority which until then had remained the prerogative of the Jews."

They reminded him of the prophecy made by the ancient patriarch Jacob, immediately before his death, when he called his sons and said:

> *Gather yourselves together, that I may tell you that which shall befall you in the last days.*
>
> *The scepter shall not depart from Judah, nor a law giver from between his feet, until Shiloh comes, and unto him shall the gathering of the people be.*

Still not satisfied, Reza had asked about the Prophet Mohammed's own words when he said, "The Mahdi will be of my own stock, broad of forehead and aquiline of nose."

The leader of the Brotherhood replied to Reza, "His father is one of us. Only his mother is a Jewess, which is part of the fulfillment of this prophecy."

Reza never again openly questioned the genealogy of Ari Ben Chaim, and what doubts persisted he kept to himself.

Reaching the ancient sanctuary, he parked and went inside. Upon seeing Ari's unkempt mane of black curly hair and untrimmed beard, he knew he had found the prophet. Even Ari's simple leather sandals fit his image of how a holy man would dress.

Reza bowed deeply before Ari then reached into his breast pocket, took out a bulging envelope, and handed it to Jamal. "*Mu'cha karem*, many thanks," he said to the Druze.

Jamal touched his lips and forehead in response and walked out without counting the money.

"You will come with me, Your Excellency," Reza said in English. "Your followers are waiting in the city,"

"Who do they think I am?" Ari mumbled to himself. Fear of what was coming kept adrenaline pumping through his veins

They drove in silence for twenty kilometers before approaching a small village surrounded by a grove of poplars. Driving through the sleeping community, they disturbed only a few stray dogs, then continued to Damascus. In the morning stillness they could hear the murmur of running water from the aqueducts watering the apricot trees that girdled Damascus.

Entering the city through the Bawabet Ullah, the Gates of God, they passed on to the maidan, the city center where shops stretched out to meet the minarets and domes set between large homes and villas.

Reza honked his horn before a wooden gate. When it opened, he drove into a graveled courtyard, stopped and stepped out of the vehicle, motioning for Ari to follow. Ari refused to get out of the vehicle. Reza gingerly took Ari's arm. "They are expecting you, Your Excellency." By now Ari didn't know what to expect, but he did know he would not go meekly to slaughter.

Entering through a small door in a narrow passage, they turned a corner and found themselves in a marble court with a fountain in the center and orange trees planted around the walls. All the rooms opened into this court. Mosaics covered the walls and water bubbled up into marble basins and flowed away by conduits.

A servant, dressed in white trousers and tunic, led Ari and Reza over a little bridge that crossed a running stream behind the main court. They were in a garden full of cultivated tulips, through which they passed to a room with a high curved ceiling.

"Who lives here?" Ari asked, unable to conceal his amazement at the signs of obvious wealth.

"This is a tekiyah," Reza replied. "A religious institution that originally housed Sufi's."

"What?" Ari asked, puzzled and even more nervous as he looked for a way to escape.

"Something like a monastery, only there is no vow of chastity here. The members may have as many wives as they choose outside the tekiyah."

A door opened and a man wearing a flowing white robe and a green turban entered the room and knelt before Ari. The man touched his forehead on the carpet, murmuring greetings in Farsi, which Reza interpreted.

"This is Abd Umar. He welcomes Your Excellency and apologizes for any inconvenience caused by rough treatment at the airport. He says those dogs, the Palestinians, could not be trusted with the knowledge of your true identity. They treated you like the enemy because they thought you were an Israeli."

"I am Israeli," Ari protested. His blood froze at the sight of this man kneeling before him.

The man in the green turban, who apparently knew no English, stood, then motioned for them to sit.

Ari sniffed at the familiar smell of stale hashish smoke but continued to stand in a defensive mode.

Reza, with beads of perspiration showing on his forehead, quickly explained that the Ayatollah Khomeini had banned Abd Umar for his apocalyptic sermons in a Tehran mosque. Umar now lived in Damascus under the guise of a Sufi and had gathered a loosely knit group around him. Reza explained that he had, himself, secretly joined the brotherhood only the previous year.

"Abd Umar has an important message for you. He tells me he has waited a lifetime for this occasion, but first you must sit and have some refreshments. It is necessary after your long journey," Reza said, pointing to a low couch.

Reluctantly, Ari sat down like a man condemned to eat his last meal. A male servant entered the room with a tray of small glasses filled with steaming hot tea steeped in mint. The servant offered a bowl of hand-cracked sugar cubes to him. Ari put up his hand to say no. The servant then passed the sugar bowl to Reza who took a large, irregular shaped piece and put it between his teeth. Then he sipped his tea through the sugar.

Ari watched as Abd Umar drank his tea in the same manner. Next came a plate of cookies made of rice flour and a tray of candy made from boiled honey and almonds. Ari passed these up also. Reza selected a yellow apple from a bowl of fruit, gracefully pared the peel off in one piece, cut the apple into thin slices and offered it to Ari with a flourish. After a second round of tea, Umar signaled, with a raised eyebrow, for the servant to clear the table and leave the room.

"Seven years will be your reign." Abd Umar spoke directly to Ari as Reza translated from Farsi to English. "You will fill the earth with right and with justice even as it has been filled with wrong and oppression."

"Where is he getting this information?" Ari asked Reza. It slowly dawned on Ari that these people believed he was the Muslim messiah they were talking about.

Reza registered no surprise at Ari's lack of knowledge on this matter. "Your holiness knows the ancient texts, but permit me to refresh your memory."

The slave-girl shall give birth to her mistress
and those who were but barefoot, naked, needy herdsmen
shall build buildings ever higher and higher.

"This is to say, in the latter days, children will disrespect their parents and chaos will appear in the social order as the sedentary way of life overcomes the nomadic way. It is even now happening in the House of Saud, keepers of the Holy Stone, even as the angel Gabriel declared."

Ari tensed at the mention of the archangel. He had never really believed Lily when she talked about the angel Michael appearing to her in dreams.

"Who did you say gave this message?" Ari mentally scrambled to make a rational connection between his kidnapping and archangels.

"Gabriel, who gave the Koran to Mohammed," Reza replied politely.

Abd Umar continued his narration. "Toward the end of your seven-year reign, a man blind in his right eye, in which all light is extinguished, even as it were a grape, will cause great corruption on earth and by his power to work marvels will win more and more men to his side. But we, the believers, will fight against him."

Ari's mind spun in wild conjecture as Reza translated this. *They intend to keep me here seven years. No way! What happens when they figure out I'm not their savior? I'm not waiting for the guy with a grape for an eye to show up.*

A sound like one long, drawn-out note of anguish pierced the air. Ari stiffened as he realized he was not the only prisoner. Neither Abd Umar nor Reza reacted in any visible manner. The cry rang out again, and then all was silent.

"What's going on?" Ari blurted.

"You heard a Sufi disciple asking God to help him in meditation. He cries out in despair, Al-lah. By this supplication, he hopes to achieve self realization with God," Reza replied.

Ari couldn't fathom the strange expression in Reza's eyes. He intuited it didn't bode well for him. "Now what's he saying?" Ari tried to mask his growing anxiety.

"He says you must be tired after your long journey and in need of the soothing waters of the hamam."

A servant led the increasingly nervous Ari to the other side of the courtyard and to the entrance of a room tiled from ceiling to floor. He pointed to a towel and motioned for Ari to disrobe.

Ari glanced at the room, which seemed to him to be designed so that blood and guts could disappear without a trace, and he balked at the doorway. "I'm not going to die like a butchered pig."

Puzzled but determined, the servant pantomimed dropping his trousers, pulling his tunic over his head, and tossing it on the floor. Then, motioning to Ari to follow suit, he wrapped a thin towel around his waist and lay stomach down on a tiled massage table.

A bald man with muscles like an Olympic wrestler entered from the opposite door. Ari stepped back as he searched for a weapon in the man's hands. Instead, he saw that his executioner carried a flask of oil.

With relief, Ari recognized what they wanted from him. Silently, he slipped off his clothes, wrapped a towel around his waist and lay face down on the low table. The delicate scent of sesame-seed oil filled the steamy room. Ari's tense muscles relaxed.

After ten minutes, the big man poured pitchers of lukewarm water over Ari's body and rubbed his skin with a soft pumice stone, causing layers of gray, dead skin to roll off. Once again, he sluiced him with clean, clear water, then led him to a pool of hot water. The water entered through one pipe and exited another, so he never sat in dirty water. One more buffing, this time with a rough cloth made of goat hair, then he sat in a pool of cool running water.

Finally, a barber came and trimmed his hair and beard. After completing the unexpected but not unpleasant ablutions, they dressed him in a new cotton tunic and flowing robe. The servant wound a green cloth turban around his head and tucked the loose end securely in place.

Before falling asleep that night, Ari analyzed the day's amazing events. It was clearly a case of mistaken identity, assuming that a character such as the Mahdi actually did exist. Why had they picked him? He reviewed what he knew about his birth. It wasn't much. On his eighteenth birthday, his father had revealed how someone discovered him in a trash bin, only a few hours old. They couldn't determine if the abandoned infant was Arab or Jew because neither group would toss away a healthy male infant, even during a war. He was adopted at age two and brought up on the kibbutz.

Years later, he met Lily, who claims that an archangel speaks to her, in the psychiatric clinic in Jerusalem. These people in Damascus seem to be on talking terms with archangels, too. *I just don't get it.*

Ari tried to place the one-eyed man in the scheme of things. Moshe Dayan was the only man he knew of who was blind in one eye. He knew Dayan had been one of the men responsible for the reunification of Jerusalem in 1967. But Dayan died in 1981, so he couldn't be the person Reza was talking about.

Jerusalem is under Jewish rule after nearly two thousand years. At the same time, an infant boy is found. The child grows up and is proclaimed the long awaited Mahdi in Damascus.

"The Muslim messiah? Me?" Ari mumbled before falling into a troubled sleep.

Chapter 6

Ari rose before dawn, determined to play the part of the mystic holy man while waiting for an opportunity to escape. He made his morning ablutions as best he could then knelt on the prayer mat facing Mecca. His captors didn't seem to know much more about how he should behave than he did. Only Reza acted uneasy when Ari showed little familiarity with traditional Muslim rites, such as the rinsing of hands, feet, and face before prayer.

"Religion is founded on cleanliness, and purification is the key to prayer," Reza instructed him in a pedantic but polite voice. "When you first rise in the morning you rinse your hands three times and say *O'God I ask thee for luck and blessing.* You then take a handful of water with your right hand and rinse your mouth three times. Then you take another handful of water and inhale it three times, forcing it with your breath up your nose, thereby flushing it out. Then say *O'God I seek refuge in thee against the stench of hell and evil in the world.*"

Ari mimicked his teacher's every move and recited each prayer exactly as he heard it spoken.

Continuing the exercise, Reza took up another handful of water for his face and washed it from the flat part of his forehead to his chin and from ear to ear. "Do this three times letting the water pour over your beard. Say *O'God cleanse thou the face of thy saints and blacken the faces of thy enemies.*"

Then he washed his arms up to his elbows three times. He continued with the washing of his ears and neck, then with fresh water washed first his right foot three times, passing his fingers between the toes from the bottom up, beginning with the little toe of the right foot and ending with the little toe of the left.

"As you wash your right foot say, *O' God, steady my foot on the narrow bridge on that day when feet slip down into the fires of hell.*" Reza then turned his head up to heaven and said, "I testify that there is no God but Allah, that he has no associate, and that Mohammed is his servant."

He continued teaching Ari. "Remember, do not wash each member more than three times. Whoever goes beyond three transgresses. Secondly, do not be extravagant with water."

After the rigors of washing, Ari found himself surprisingly hungry when the servants brought in a large round tray. He stuffed flat bread and soft goat's cheese into his mouth while Reza continued the lessons

"The Prophet said that when a Muslim rinses his mouth, the sin leaves it; when he blows his nose, sin is gone; and when he washes his hands, sins are removed. Of course your holiness knows no sin. I tell you this that you will not offend the sensibilities of lesser minds." Reza looked pointedly at the servants standing in the shadows.

"When you stand to pray, remember to raise your hands so high that the whiteness of your armpits can be seen. At the end of your supplication wipe your face with your hands like this." He lightly pressed the palms of his hands over his face in demonstration.

Ari wiped his face with his palms and nodded.

"When you look into a mirror thank God who has given nobility and beauty to the form of your face."

Barely pausing, Reza continued, "When you go to sleep at night, first perform the ablutions then rest on your right side. Then say *Allah akbar*, God is Great, thirty-four times, then *glory be to God*, thirty-three times, followed by *praise be to God* thirty-three times."

When Ari could eat no more, the servants cleared the table. He and Reza crossed through the garden. The light sweet scent of orange blossoms made Ari homesick for his family. With great effort he pushed away the thought that they were dead, vowing to deal with his grief when he made it back home.

That night he dreamed about Lily. She held his hand and led him through a dense forest. Low hanging branches tore at his shirt as they stooped beneath fragrant fir boughs. They came out of the trees into a clearing overlooking the sleeping city of Jerusalem. The fragile sliver of moon cast an eerie light.

Lily slipped her left arm around Ari's waist, standing so close he could feel the rise and fall of her labored breathing. He encircled her in his arms, as if to comfort and protect her from the evil he felt brooding over Jerusalem.

Chapter 7

Friday, all the male population of Damascus, dressed in their best apparel, paraded in the streets on their way to the Great Mosque. Ari was not the only one to wear the green turban of the *Seyyed*, signifying the descendants of the Imam.

He made mental notes of the different shops, the sweets sellers, the second-hand clothing stores, and the eating shops where the aroma of roasting meats poured out to mingle in the dust-laden air. This was his first opportunity outside the mansion, and he tried to miss nothing that would aid in his escape.

Reza had drilled him in the rituals again. "When you arrive at the mosque and are about to enter it, say, *O' God, forgive me all my sins and open for me the doors of your mercy*. Then step forward with your right foot first."

At the Great Mosque, they left their shoes with a crippled attendant by the entrance and wandered into the cloister that ran along the whole west side of the mosque. Ari saw that a fire had robbed the mosque of much of its former beauty. He saw traces of what looked like an ancient church embedded in the walls and gates. The court was half in shadow and half in sunlight. Little boys with green willow switches in their hands, ran about in play, nearly knocking Reza and Ari off their feet.

Ari forced himself not to smile as he thought of the similarity between them and Jewish children scrambling around the synagogue on the Sabbath.

After performing the prerequisite ablutions in the public fountain, the faithful made their first prostrations before entering the mosque. Ari and Reza did likewise, followed them in, and watched them fall into lines from east to west.

The chant of the Imam began when they had assembled to the number of three or four hundred. "*Allah,*" they cried in Arabic. The congregation, Ari included, fell with a single movement upon their faces, and remained a full minute in silent adoration until the high chant began again.

> *The Creator of this world and the next, of the heavens and of the earth. He who leads the righteous in the true path and the wicked to destruction—Allah!*

As the name Allah echoed through the colonnades, the listeners prostrated themselves again. For a moment all the sanctuary was silent.

Back in the tekiyah, Ari felt bold and asked Reza a direct question. "What do you know about my birth?"

Reza appeared startled, then a shadow crossed his face. The usually animated man became subdued. "I have some knowledge about your father, a *Seyyed* from a prominent family in Qom. Iran sent him to the West Bank to serve as a spiritual guide for Hamas. He died the same year you were born, but not before he forwarded certain documents to Tehran concerning the birth of a son. By the time they traced you to the Baby Home in Jerusalem, the adoption had taken place. For reasons never explained, you were allowed to grow up on a communal farm, or kibbutz as you call it."

"What about my mother? Who was she?" Ari asked, trying to appear indifferent.

"I know nothing more." Reza ended the conversation by turning and leaving the room.

Clearly he did not want to talk about Ari's father or mother, and that puzzled Ari. He felt Reza was holding something back. However, Ari didn't intend to stick around long enough to unravel the puzzle. He needed to visit Moshe and Shifra's grave and pay his respect to their memory. They were the only parents he knew, and they had been good to him. His original intention on returning to Israel was to ask Lily to marry him. *How had it come to this? I have to get out of Damascus.*

That night he decided to leave. It wasn't a matter of escape. They believed him to be the Hidden Imam, who could come and go in time and space by an act of occultation. Therefore, Ari had been free to move about the tekiyah. Still, he intended to be far from the tekiyah before they discovered his absence.

Two hours before dawn, when the night air was at its coolest and sleep at its deepest, Ari slipped out of his chamber and crept through the garden with the marble fountains. Hearing footsteps he froze. He waited until the night crickets resumed their gentle chirping. Silently, like a cat, he climbed the lower branches of an orange tree, then scaled the wall. Balancing on the edge, he caught a glimpse of a man, possibly Reza, passing between two trees.

Jumping to the soft earth he ran fast, turning and twisting his way through the narrow alleyway. He made his way to the central maidan that he recognized by the landmark Hotel Victoria. On a hunch, he slipped around to the loading dock in back of the hotel's kitchen.

As he anticipated, peasants were unloading crates of cucumbers, tomatoes, and onions. He saw live chickens, tied together at the feet, hanging upside down on a pole. Great barrels of olives and crocks of cheese in salt water stood in one corner.

When the farmers' backs were turned, he slipped into the back of a truck, crouching behind empty crates. When the owner of the truck finished his business, he drank a hot glass of tea with the other men, then returned to his vehicle.

Peering through a crack in the side panels, Ari saw that the driver wore the headdress of a Druze. He smiled, knowing it meant he would be heading for the Golan. The truck took off at an excruciatingly slow speed. Just before they turned the corner, Ari saw Reza running up to the loading dock.

Ari felt good about eluding Reza without a confrontation. Basic training in the Israeli Army gave him the skills to break Reza's neck with ease. The thought of executing that fatal blow, cracking Reza's absurdly thin neck with the protruding Adam's apple, sent waves of nausea surging through his body.

Unimpeded, the truck left Damascus and headed west. Ari saw the soft soil of the desert come to an end and the beginning of volcanic rocks. A great plain stretched to the foot of Mount Hermon in an unbroken expanse, completely deserted, almost devoid of vegetation and strewn with black volcanic stones. The truck came to a crossroads and rolled to a near stop before turning north. Ari chose this moment to jump from the vehicle, hitting the road in a crouch, then rolling behind a rock formation to avoid being seen.

As the dust from the truck faded into the distance, he stood up and surveyed the landscape before him. The southern end of the lava bed lay on the left like a frozen black sea.

Sun and frost and eons of time had rent the lava bed and obliterated the the hills. He saw that one or two terebinth bushes had found a foothold in the crevices, but they were bare and gray and did nothing to counter the general sense of lifelessness.

Ari followed a track that led him straight through that desolate land. The edge of the lava plateau stood a few feet above the plain. Here the stones lay so close together, there was no room for even the slenderest of plants. Ari picked up a smooth black stone worn down by water. The morning sun shimmered above the lava, making it look like a sheet of molten metal.

Ari glanced at the angle of the sun knowing he would have to make it through the lava bed before the pitiless heat made it unendurable. At first, he was not aware of the minute paths that intersected the lava because they were so small and faint. As he crossed the bleak expanse, he realized that hundreds of generations of passing feet had pushed aside the cinder blocks ever so little, making it possible to travel through that wilderness of stone.

The sun was overhead before he reached the brink of the lava hills and caught a sight of the gray tower of a shrine in the plain below. He picked up a smooth pebble and sucked it to relieve the dryness in his mouth. The parched air absorbed his perspiration before he had time to wipe his neck. He made for the shrine, hoping it would contain a stone basin of water like the shrine where he first met Reza.

He entered through a doorway carved with flowing scrolls and flowers. There on the floor was a basin, filled to the brim. Gratefully, he fell to his knees and gulped water from his cupped hand.

Ari rested in the shelter of the shrine, taking stock of his options. The most direct route would lead to the no-man's-land between Syria and Israel. Ari knew the United Nations peacekeeping force had their headquarters there. He also knew the

UN soldiers had no love for Israel and were likely to turn him over to the Syrian army. If he headed north towards Mount Hermon, he would have to evade Syrian troop movements but would have a better chance of meeting an Israeli patrol on the western slopes of the mountain.

He weighed his chances of persuading UN soldiers to allow him to cross into Israel. Shaking his head, he turned north towards the snow-capped peaks of Hermon. Walking at twice his previous speed, now that he was out of the treacherous lava beds, he reached the lower slopes before sunset.

Syrian patrols made only cursory inspection along the border, confident that infiltrators would not come from Israel into Syria. Ari easily avoided their bunkers as he approached a barbed-wire fence, which indicated he had reached Israel's border. On the other side he saw a wide swath of earth, carefully graded and raked.

As he anticipated, within an hour, Israeli soldiers came looking for footprints in the smooth soil.

He picked up a large stone and hurled it at the fence, then hid himself behind a boulder. The Israeli patrol cautiously approached the area. Two men got out of the jeep in the fading twilight and looked for footprints in the soft dirt.

Ari cautiously waved a hand above the boulder and called out in Hebrew. "*Havre*, comrades! Over here."

The driver switched off the jeep's lights and hit the ground in one smooth motion. The other two took cover in a culvert. "Ambush!" They shouted to each other.

"Don't be afraid! I'm not armed!" Ari called out. "My name's Ari Ben Chaim. I've been kidnapped and held in Damascus."

He could hear an animated debate between the men on the other side of the fence. One thought it a trap. Another argued that no Arab could speak Hebrew with that inflection.

"I'm coming out with my hands above my head." Ari cautiously showed himself, then walked ten paces to the fence.

After another heated argument, a soldier took a pair of wire cutters out of the jeep and cut the two bottom wires. "I just put the entire Northern Command on alert," he said.

Even as he spoke, red lights, indicating that a terrorist had infiltrated the border, blinked on in the command post on Mount Hermon. Helicopters and ground patrol units would spread over the Golan Heights and the Galilee. Civilian communities went on alert as mothers in moshavim, kibbutzim, and towns as far away as Kiryat Shmona sent their children to spend the night in their fortified safe rooms.

"*Y'allah*, get moving." The soldier motioned to Ari to crawl through the fence. "We don't want our buddies up there in the bunker to shoot you."

The driver of the jeep radioed back to his commanding officer. "Yeah, calm down. We cut the wire. We have a man claiming to be an Israeli." The driver got behind the wheel of his jeep and turned on the motor. "Let's get him in before they finish supper over there," he said while glancing in the direction of the Syrian bunker on the opposite hill.

Chapter 8

They took Ari to the military command post in the Northern Galilee and left him in a wooden shack that served as a debriefing room. The room was cold and damp and smelled like old shoes, but he felt safe and sat down on a straight-backed chair and stretched his legs out.

The door opened and a tall, bald man with a bushy red beard entered the room. "Motti Pincus, Mossad," he said, identifying himself as an agent of the Israeli intelligence service. Pincus neither smiled nor offered his hand.

Ari nodded as if in agreement that the man was who he said he was.

The one-sided introduction over, Agent Pincus settled his lanky frame in the inadequate chair, reached in his jacket, then took out a small notebook and pen. As he held the pen in his slender fingers, the setting sun glinting through the dirt-streaked window highlighted the freckles on his hands.

"You say you were kidnapped by Arabs at Ben Gurion, driven to Damascus by a Druze, and treated with respect and kindness by a Shi'ite mullah. Then you escaped and crossed the lava beds on foot. Why can't I believe you?" He roughly pushed his chair back scratching the floor.

Ari tried to reply, but Pincus held up his hand with fingers and thumb pinched together to indicate *hold that thought.*

"The psychiatrist who treated you after the Abu Tur incident was murdered with the same type of weapon as that used on your parents." Pincus paused for a moment, wrote something in his notebook, then looked directly in Ari's eyes. "Who were your accomplices?"

Shaking, Ari reached for a pack of cigarettes in his shirt pocket, as his numb brain tried to make sense of the accusation. *Dr. Rosen dead? They think I did it? What does his death have to do with the death of my parents?* Questions with no answers made his head ache while he searched his pockets for matches. *Was Reza connected to his parents' death?*

Pincus leaned over the desk and offered him a light from his own lighter.

"Murder my parents? What motive would I have?" Ari's fingers trembled as he took a deep drag, shortening his cigarette by a third. The ashes fell unnoticed on the bare floor.

"Motive? You resented your adopted parents for committing you to a psychiatric clinic. Rosen refused to give you a release from further army service. He explicitly states in his evaluation that you are not insane. The cook? Mistakenly killed in place of Rosen's partner. Assassins could have been hired in India."

What cook? Ari's mind raced with questions. *How many were dead?*

"Would I return to Israel and fake being kidnapped?" Ari smashed his stub in the ashtray. "I should have killed Reza when I had the chance."

"What?" Pincus looked up sharply.

"Nothing."

Pincus interrogated Ari all morning, but failed to get a confession or make him vary his story. As a last resort, he brought in Ira Stern, an Israeli Army psychiatrist.

Stern had treated hundreds of soldiers. His unit, positioned behind the lines in times of war, treated soldiers in a state of shock. Then, while still on the front, he returned them to their fighting unit.

He gazed intently at Ari and thought, if he put a *kaffiyeh* on the young man, he'd look like an Arab with his heavy Semitic features, curly black hair, eyebrows one bushy line over a hawk-like nose, the lips full but finely outlined.

"According to your file, your birth parents are unknown. Is that correct?" Dr. Stern, a middle-aged man with a pronounced paunch, spoke in soft tones. He wanted to know as many details about Ari's history as possible.

"Tossed away at birth—found in a trash bin." Ari suddenly remembered what Reza had told him about his birth father—an Iranian from the holy city of Qom. He chose not to share that bit of biography with this Army shrink.

"Tell me about the Abu Tur incident," Dr. Stern said after a lengthy silence.

"That's water under the bridge, as far as I'm concerned," Ari replied, knowing that would not deter the doctor.

"I'm only interested insofar as this incident led to your nervous breakdown and eventual treatment with Dr. Rosen."

"It's all in my file."

"I want to hear it in your own words. Bear with me Ari. I have your welfare in mind, not your destruction."

Ari sighed with relief that the doctor did not question him about Damascus. He did not want to talk about what had happened in Abu Tur either, but he felt he had no choice.

He spoke in a low voice as if talking to himself. "My unit was deployed to Abu Tur. I drove the lead jeep. The first rock smashed my windshield as I entered the village square. We had orders to blow up a certain house for harboring a terrorist. It's usually the parents' home. The young men defied orders to return to their houses."

"Teenage males?" Dr. Stern asked.

Ari nodded.

"Where were the adult men of the village?"

"Already in custody."

"The boys refused to obey and continued hurling rocks. How did that make you feel?"

Ari stared at the psychiatrist. "Like beating the crap out of them. Instead, we tied their hands with zip ties and forced them to lie face down on the ground. I can still smell the stink of fear that poured from their bodies. The only sound I heard was the distant drone of a fighter jet streaking up the Jordan Valley. I could see the worried faces of the women at their windows."

"Whose idea was it to bury them alive?"

Ari shook his head as if ridding his brain of unwanted images. He looked at the floor, as he continued. "The lieutenant ordered the guy on the bulldozer to do it, but the driver walked away. It all happened so fast. The lieutenant finally jumped on the seat of the bulldozer and piled the dirt on."

"Did anyone try to stop him?"

"Of course, doors flew open and the mothers scrabbled through the dirt with their bare hands. Their sons sat up coughing and gasping for air. They wiped the tears and mucous off with their head scarves."

"Did you try to stop them?" Dr. Stern scribbled quietly on his notepad without looking up.

"What do you think? We don't shoot women. What I did do was hand my weapon to my commanding officer. '*Kach oto*, take it,' I said. I quit."

Dr. Stern made a few more notes, then suggested they break for lunch. After the doctor left the shack, a soldier brought Ari a tray with turkey schnitzel and rice. He gulped it down, surprised by his appetite.

Dr. Stern came back with two cups of strong, hot coffee and continued the session. To Ari's discomfort, he insisted on a recapitulation of everything that happened from the time his plane landed at Ben Gurion Airport.

"Take your time, I've got all afternoon."

By evening, Dr. Stern felt Ari was telling some of the truth, but at the same time holding back vital information. He wrote in his report that it was in the realm of possibility that this sect believed Ari to be their so-called messiah, the Twelfth Imam, or Mahdi.

Motti Pincus' final report suggested there was not any concrete evidence to link Ari to the four murders. He ended with a recommendation that Army Intelligence consider using Ari as a double agent.

They released him Friday afternoon shortly after the buses stopped running for the Sabbath. Dressed in borrowed jeans and tee-shirt, Ari hitched a ride to the main highway running north and south. This took him to the crossroads near his kibbutz.

Ari jumped over a wooden fence and crossed the horse pasture. When he reached the center of his kibbutz he could see Sabbath candles flickering in the communal dining room. Tears, long held in check, welled up as he thought of his mother and father. He put his foot on the steps leading to the dining room, then abruptly turned and walked toward the grove of eucalyptus on the outer perimeter of the settlement. In the weak moonlight he searched for the headstone of his adopted parents, Moshe and Shifra Ben Chaim. When he found them, he knelt on the soft soil, already covered with new grass, and wept. As he placed two pebbles on the headstone, he vowed he would avenge their deaths. He and the Brotherhood would meet again, of that he was certain. But he would be in control this time.

Chapter 9

As a *ben meshak*, son of the kibbutz, Ari received a guarded welcome at Kibbutz Shoshanat HaEmekim. The commune's sorrow over the brutal murders of Shifra and Moshe had washed away any resentment that members held against Ari for his role in the Abu Tur incident. But the kibbutz had paid for his psychiatric care, and had expected him to return home when he was discharged from Bet Shalom. The older members, who had lived through four wars, thought his extended travels to India an indulgence. His contemporaries secretly admired him.

Ari could not slip back into the rhythm and daily routine of the commune. He rose while it was still dark and compulsively chain smoked, filling the ashtray in his parents' cottage. Along with thoughts of revenge, the accusation of Motti Pincus filled every waking moment and even his dreams.

Murderer.

He recalled with horror the goat's slit neck spurting blood over the threshold on his arrival at the tekiyah. Qorban, ritual sacrifice. Did they sacrifice his parents in the same way?

And Dr. Rosen? What was the connection? Did Rosen's partner, Heftsibah Klein, believe Ari was responsible?

Worse yet, did Lily believe he was capable of murder? He had to find the answers.

The sun rose over the Golan and workers scattered to their duties. In the nursery, baby nurses stripped the infants of their soggy nightclothes, then bathed and dressed them before their mothers came for the first morning kisses. The workers who gathered the rose petals in the pre-dawn were in the dining room for the first breakfast shift.

Ari searched the communal dining room for Noam, the kibbutz chairman, and found him sitting by the window drinking *cafe botz*, thick coffee.

"*Ah-lan*," said Noam, using a common Arabic expression popular with the sabras.

Ari stiffened and deliberately replied in formal Hebrew, "*Boker tov*, good morning."

Noam then replied in like manner, "*Boker or*, light of the morning."

Ari spoke bluntly. "I need to know who murdered my parents and why."

Noam put down his coffee cup, spilling a few drops. "What are you proposing?" He spoke in the slow deliberate manner of a man who feared little in life.

"I want to go to Jerusalem to see Dr. Klein."

"What's the connection?" Noam's shaggy eyebrows rose.

By Noam's response, Ari understood he knew nothing about the murder of Dr. Rosen and the cook.

"I just need to talk to her," Ari said without elaboration.

"I'm not going to receive a bill from her, I hope. I don't begrudge paying for psychiatric treatment. The kibbutz has the money, but it's the principle. After six months of expensive treatment, you took off for India. What kind of cure is that?"

Ari snorted, causing heads to turn in his direction. "I need answers about the murder of my parents."

"You always have a home here, Ari, you know that." Noam stood and put his gnarled arms around the younger man's shoulder. "Go in peace."

Ari chose a window seat on the bus ride up to Jerusalem. There wasn't much to see after they passed the Sea of Galilee and crossed over the narrow Jordan River. The landscape in the Jordan Valley was as barren and desolate as a moonscape, save for the occasional fields of tomatoes and cucumbers cultivated by drip irrigation.

Then he remembered the letter Noam had given him just before he left the kibbutz. When he saw that it was from a solicitor in England, he had put it away to read privately. Now was the time, he decided. He pulled it out of his pack. Inside the heavy white envelope he found a brief note, along with a smaller blue envelope. He opened the second envelope and took out a single sheet of tissue-thin blue paper and read.

Dear Ari,

I have arranged for you to read this after my death. My name means nothing to you now, but do you remember the poster above your cot in the Baby Home? I would point to the picture of the little boy and you would say, in English, "Christopher Robin." You impressed the other Hebrew-speaking nurses.

I'm sure you now know the truth about your origins. Israel was surrounded on all sides and people were afraid. Your mother abandoned you immediately after birth. The other nurses considered you the enemy and seldom touched you. I fell in love with your curly hair and your skin the color of cafe au lait. You had a little scar on your cheek. I thought the birthmark looked like a lion cub, which is why I named you Ari. I massaged your spine and exercised your legs. The doctor said you would never have walked if I hadn't come into your life at that critical moment.

In the enclosed pictures you can see your first birthday, celebrated with a chocolate cake and one fat candle.

The day your new parents took you to their home, you can see me in the picture holding a bouquet of roses from their kibbutz. Your expression in the photo is happy and unconcerned for the future, but you cried when they drove out the garden gate. You turned to look back at me and screamed when you realized I was not coming with you.

Your adopted parents, Moshe and Shifra, asked me not to communicate with you, so you could bond with them.

I respected their wishes, but I have never forgotten you.

With love,

Sheila Queller

Ari's chest tightened and his breath came in uneven gulps as he stared at the photographs. Desperate for air, he struggled to open the stuck window, which caused the passenger in front of him to turn and stare. He stuck his head out the window and sucked in fresh air.

The bus stopped at a kiosk ten minutes outside Jericho. Most of the passengers got off to buy juice or cold soft drinks.

Still feeling distraught from the contents of the letter, Ari remained in his seat with one hand over his eyes, feigning sleep. Fragments of an English nursery rhyme echoed in his head. He searched his memory for a face to place with Nurse Queller's name. Nothing. To his mounting chagrin, he found he had no memories of his life before the children's house on the kibbutz.

His fellow passengers noisily reboarded the bus. As the driver pulled away from the curb, Ari turned and looked out the back window at the overgrown bougainvillea bushes blazing a brilliant fuchsia. Without warning he found himself in a flashback to his childhood, looking out a back window, screaming in terror. Someone he loved was waving good-bye. *Could it have been Miss Queller?*

Feeling sick in the pit of his stomach, he groaned, and the passenger next to him asked if he was all right. "*Col beseder*, everything is fine," he replied even though he felt anything but.

On the ascent from Jericho to Jerusalem, Ari tried to dismiss the growing realization that this British nurse might have died because of her connection to him. His parents, Dr. Rosen and now this. What did the killing of an elderly English woman serve? How many more would this twisted group in Damascus sacrifice?

The woman in the adjoining seat offered him a section of freshly peeled orange. The sweet scent of citric oil pricked his nostrils, but he refused.

All he could think about now was Lily. *She too could be in danger because of me.* He glanced around the crowded bus at his fellow passengers. *Am I being followed*?

When the bus pulled into Jerusalem's central bus station he waited until all the passengers had gathered their bundles and parcels and left the bus.

"Hey, *Gingi*, wake up! We're in Jerusalem," the driver said, as he walked down the aisle on a routine bomb sweep.

Ari grabbed his knapsack from the overhead rack and went to mix in with the crowd in the station.

Chapter 10

The village of Ain Karem, nestled in a wadi on the southwest slopes of Jerusalem, lay approximately a half day's walk from the Temple Mount. Two buildings stood sentinel over the village, Hadassah Hospital on the hilltop to the west and Yad VaShem, the memorial to the Holocaust, to the east.

Ari slipped into Bet Shalom without being detected. He went straight to Dr. Klein's office and paused outside the half-opened door. After he determined that the doctor was alone, he entered just as she ground her cigarette stub into the ashtray. She looked up, startled, quickly composed herself, and gripped Ari's extended hand.

"*Barukh haba*, welcome is he who comes," said Dr. Klein with a guarded expression. Like most secular Jews she didn't complete the saying with "in the name of the Lord."

Ari sat in a chair and smiled broadly in visible relief at finding Dr. Klein alive and safe. He mentally vowed to keep it that way.

In his straightforward manner, he started at the beginning and related everything since his abduction. Two hours later, at Dr. Klein's suggestion, they adjourned to the kitchen for coffee.

"You knew our cook was murdered the same night as Dr. Rosen?" Her expression did not change, but her knuckles turned white as she poured the thick Turkish coffee into little cups.

Ari did know about the cook. With bitterness he recalled how the Mossad agent had accused him. He said nothing of this to Dr. Klein. Instead, he decided to read her the letter from Nurse Queller.

Dr. Klein's face looked drained after Ari read the letter from the British nurse. "They're killing everyone close to you," she said quietly.

Ari nodded.

"Why do you think they have picked you as their messiah?" Dr. Klein's hands shook as she opened a new carton of cigarettes.

"My biological father was from Qom." Ari choked on the word father.

"Where's Qom?" Dr. Klein asked. She picked up a pack of *Time*, shook one out, struck a match, lit the cigarette, and inhaled.

"One hundred miles from Tehran. All the big guys in the Iranian revolution hang out there, sort of a university town for Muslim priests. My father was an emissary, sent from the mullahs in Qom to instruct the newly formed Hamas."

"They've been tracking you since you left the orphanage?" Dr. Klein's face looked grim. "They could still be on your trail."

Ari shrugged his shoulders. "Reza implied that the Mahdi is infallible, able to come and go as he pleases. Don't ask me what that means. It could be astral travel for all I know. Anyway, it was hard work trekking through those lava beds."

"O.K., so you're not their pope," Dr. Klein said. "What are we going to do with you now? Were you followed?"

"No. I took precautions." He stared out the window at the trees. "I took the bus from the main station to Hadassah Hospital, then ducked down several hallways and joined a group of tourists at the Chagall window. I made sure nobody was following me when I hiked down the hill into Ain Karem."

"Shin Bet has had the clinic under surveillance since the murders," Dr. Klein said matter-of-factly.

"I may be crazy but I'm not stupid." Ari smiled at his own joke, trying to break the tension in the smoke-filled kitchen.

"I climbed the outer wall of the Russian convent next door. Then I rolled under the barbed wire fence in the thicket that separates the two properties."

"You aren't safe here, but I've got an idea. You remember Hamed, the gardener here at Bet Shalom?"

"Yeah, I remember him," Ari replied.

"He owes me," said Dr. Klein. "Last year I intervened with the military governor when they threatened to blow up Hamed's house. They suspected his son was a member in a terrorist cell. Because of me, the boy turned himself in and cleared his name. Hamed's home still stands. He lives in an isolated village west of Bet Lehem. You'd be safe there for a few days."

Ari agreed that he should go underground, but on one condition. "I want to see Lily before I disappear again."

"Impossible. I'll tell her you're safe and back in Israel." She blew smoke towards the ceiling. "Too dangerous for her."

Ari reluctantly agreed not to go to Lily. He knew the doctor's plan to hide in an isolated village was the only prudent option.

"Hamed insists on sleeping in the gatehouse since Samuel's passing. I can't make him believe I'm not afraid to be alone at night. He rigged up a buzzer system with a button in my office, one in my bedroom and another in the kitchen." Dr. Klein reached under the wooden table and pressed the hidden bell.

Two minutes later, Hamed slipped his key in the back door of the kitchen. He carried a razor sharp pruning hook in his hands. His gray hair was cropped short under a smooth-fitting skull cap. Fine lines around the outer corner of his eyes revealed a man who spent much of his time out-of-doors. The run to the kitchen left him out of breath and panting.

"I'm all right," said Dr. Klein. But there is someone here to see you."

"*Ah-lan*, welcome!" Hamed's eyes lit up when he recognized Ari.

Ari stood and awkwardly pounded Hamed on the shoulder by way of greeting. "*Keffic*, how are you?"

"*Al hamdul'allah*, praise Allah."

Dr. Klein explained to Hamed that Ari needed a place to stay where no one would recognize him.

"Like your home," she said looking directly at the gardener.

Hamed showed no reaction, but he remained silent for a long moment. The clock on the stove ticked loudly.

"My wife has never met a Jew. She and my daughters have never left our village, not even to Bet Lehem," he said in a quiet voice.

"Think it over. If you agree, the two of you can leave for your village in the morning," Dr. Klein said.

"I'll meet you at the top of the hill just before dawn? *Quais*, All right?" Ari looked at Hamed's face, knowing he would agree.

Hamed sighed deeply and said, "*En sha'allah*, Allah's will be done."

Chapter 11

Red anemones covered the Judean hillside. Purple and white cyclamen grew in the rocky outcroppings, seeming to thrive on nothing but air. Ari reached down and picked a sprig of wild garlic alongside the trail and inhaled its pungent but pleasant aroma.

Walking at a leisurely pace, Ari and Hamed covered the distance between Ain Karem and Hamed's village in a short time. The trail, used exclusively by shepherds, wound around the curves of the hillside, avoiding the outskirts of Jerusalem to the north.

Hamed's house, located outside the village on two *dunum* of land, stood near a stand of olive trees. On the south side of the house Ari saw a winter garden with giant cauliflower heads and purple eggplants. Beyond the vegetables he noted the bare trunks of pruned grape vines.

As they drew near the house, two young men approached on the path. They wore blue jeans and old leather jackets, with red-and-white checked kaffiyehs draped around their necks.

"*Salaam alechem,*" Hamed said.

"*Alechem salaam,*" they replied. Their gaze lingered on Ari's army-issue boots, then returned to his face.

Ari said nothing, knowing his Hebrew accent would identify him as an Israeli, if his boots had not already betrayed him.

Hamed and Ari continued down the path until two barking dogs approached. With one word of command from Hamed, the dogs turned and walked to the rear of the house, their heads high with pride of a job well done.

"*Ahlan wa salaam*, welcome to my home," Hamed said. They entered a hallway and Hamed slipped his shoes off at the entrance to the guest room. Ari did the same, but it took him longer to untie the laces of his boots. Brown and black tribal carpets covered the floor. A low divan piled with cushions stood against one wall. A bowl of oranges sat on the brass table in the middle of the room. Hamed motioned for Ari to sit on the low settee before he left the room.

Stacked mattresses and quilts in the corner indicated the room was also used for sleeping, probably by the unmarried daughters, Ari thought. He felt uneasy about displacing them, even for one night.

After a long wait, the door opened and Hamed returned. His wife followed him, carrying a small tray with steaming glasses of tea. She wore her long hair pulled back in a single braid covered by a white scarf and a black cotton robe with a yoke embroidered in red and gold thread. She averted her eyes as Hamed introduced her by simply saying her name, Nagia.

Ari awkwardly stood up and bowed slightly, not knowing whether to offer his hand or not. The fragrance of mint tea filled the room as she placed the tray on the table and left without a word.

"Nagia is shy with strangers. She has never seen a Jew before today."

Ari accepted the tea handed to him. "But your village is only a few kilometers from Bet Lehem. Many Israelis shop there."

"You are correct, Bet Lehem is full of Jews on Saturday, but my wife has never set foot outside this village. Our women prefer to stay at home."

After they drank tea and ate oranges, Hamed told Ari about his long struggle to build his house.

"I labored for more than eight years to build the first story. When my sons still clung to their mother's skirt, I dug out the basement, with rubber buckets made from discarded tires. I laid the foundation of stonework, picking the stones from the fields. Using skills learned from my father's father, I used little cement. By choosing the right size of each stone, I assured that this home will stand for hundreds of years. As you can see, the walls are three feet thick with recessed windows. They keep out the summer heat and the winter cold."

"A real fortress you have here," Ari said. "These walls could keep out intruders." *Like those two young men I met coming in, Ari thought to himself.*

Hamed nodded then continued with his recitation. "The work began on a second floor when Riad and Saleh were old enough to work and contribute their earnings."

"Where do your sons work?" Ari asked. He wondered where they were now and what they would say when they found him in their home.

"Saleh cuts up vegetables in a falafel stand in the central bus station. Riad works on a construction site in one of the new Jewish suburbs. On the Jews' Sabbath, they work at home helping me."

"Where are they now?" Ari could not help asking.

"Don't worry, you won't meet them. They are temporarily staying with my brother in Ramallah. Ya' Allah, I warned them. Don't antagonize the soldiers. You can't do a day's work with your arm or leg in a plaster cast."

"What are you saying?" Ari seemed puzzled.

Hamed explained to his guest how men from his village came back with broken limbs after interrogation at the military headquarters.

Ari's face showed no reaction, but his thoughts were racing. He knew the army blew up houses of Palestinians suspected of belonging to a terrorist cell. He found it hard to believe Israeli soldiers deliberately broke arms and legs. Remembering the Abu Tur incident, he said nothing.

The sun moved in the overhead position in the pale winter sky. Nagia returned and served her husband and his guest the noon meal, starting with hot pita and salads.

"Try this eggplant pickled in olive oil and vinegar. Dip your bread," Hamed suggested. Then Nagia placed a round tin tray on the low table with chicken and cauliflower sautéed in onions and butter and served over mounds of rice.

"Why don't your wife and children join us?" Ari asked as he filled his plate with food.

"They are eating the same food as you and I, but in the kitchen. You can be sure you are being discussed in much detail," Hamed replied.

As he ate with Hamed, Ari felt more relaxed than he had in a long time, even though he knew this sense of peace wouldn't last long. A slight smile on his face caused Hamed to smile back.

"Yes, my wife is a good cook," Hamed said, mistaking Ari's smile of relief as a compliment on his wife's food.

Chapter 12

"Lily, I have good news for you. Ari has escaped and he's back in Israel." Dr. Klein spoke in her usual calm, modulated voice, but the furrows on her brow revealed her uneasiness.

Ignoring the palpable signs of tension in the doctor's face, Lily impetuously threw her arms around her.

"Before you get too emotional," the doctor said, taking a step back, "you should know that he's gone into hiding."

"You saw him? Spoke to him? Why didn't you come get me?"

"Frankly, Lily, I didn't know you two were . . ."

"Lovers? I don't tell you everything. Neither does Ari." Lily felt a flicker of guilt at her exaggeration. *We soon will be lovers*, she thought with mounting joy.

Dr. Klein paused. A quizzical expression crossed her round, pleasant face. Then she sat in the chair behind her desk.

"Did he say anything about me?" Lily's voice rose with anticipation.

"Tell Lily to wait for me. Those were his exact words."

Lily felt torn between joy that Ari was safe and numb disbelief that he hadn't contacted her. Questions tumbled out in a torrent of mixed emotions.

"Where has he been all this time? Where is he now? When can I see him?"

"It isn't safe for you to know."

Accurately assessing from the guarded look on Dr. Klein's face that she would get no information from her, Lily sucked in her breath and held it. This session, the first since Dr. Rosen's death, would not go smoothly. She felt betrayed and didn't bother to hide it, releasing the air in her lungs with force.

"Lily, please sit down."

Lily glared at the doctor and remained standing.

"Suit yourself. You may stand if you wish. But let me warn you, this may be a long session. We're not here to discuss Ari. It's time to get on with your therapy. I want to hear in your own words about your encounter with the archangel."

"It's all in Dr. Rosen's file," Lily replied.

"I've read that. I need to hear it from you."

"Where do I start?" Lily sounded sarcastic.

"At the beginning. And please sit."

Lily shrugged, still standing. She desperately thought of ways to stall, but nothing came to mind. Reluctantly, she began her recital. "You think I'm crazy, that it was a hallucination, but Michael the archangel did speak to me."

"Don't presume to know what I am thinking. And crazy isn't a word in my vocabulary," Dr. Klein said in a tired but kindly voice. "Go on."

Lily sniffed in mild defiance, still inwardly reeling from the news about Ari. "When did it start? The first encounter was in Far Rockaway, New York. I was asleep when I heard my name. I sat up and there he was, shining like the sun and moon, all rolled into one. Robes grew out of his body in flowing folds that moved with him. His hair was short and curly like a lamb's. He held something like a scroll or a book in his hands.

"'Lily,' he said, quiet and dignified, 'I have an assignment for you.'

"I nearly fainted. Good thing I was in bed. You don't know

how you'll react until it happens to you. His presence filled my bedroom. I was riveted to the bed."

"'Lily,' he said. 'I have been sent to you by the Master. You will save your people from destruction.'"

"What did this angel look like?" Dr. Klein asked. Her tone suggested that nothing a patient said could surprise her.

"He had the appearance of a man but his skin glowed like transparent gold, and his robe grew out of his body," she replied.

"I see." The doctor wrote quickly in a small notebook then looked up again. "Lily, please sit down."

Lily straightened her shoulders and continued standing. She caught a glimpse of her reflection in the antique mirror above the doctor's desk. She saw a tall, young woman with a head of curly, untidy hair. Lily smiled at her own reflection.

Dr. Klein resettled her large frame in the Morris chair and pursed her lips. Her thick gray hair curled over the collar of her white smock and her pockets bulged with the packets of gum she kept on hand in her futile battle to quit smoking.

Dr. Klein specialized in identity disorders. This had brought her to the attention of Dr. Bar-El. He occasionally sent patients to her who suffered from the Jerusalem Syndrome, the divine madness that touches Christian and Jewish pilgrims every year. People like Lily, who see Jerusalem as the place closest to God.

Dr. Klein leaned back and scratched the back of her head. "We must keep this vision of yours in perspective. It's not a true psychosis in the clinical sense."

"Doctor Rosen believed me." Lily's voice took on a defiant edge.

"My dear, he found your history intriguing, but he never believed you were in communication with an archangel. You say Michael showed up in Far Rockaway. All right, that's as good a place as any. In my opinion, Jerusalem is overrated."

Chapter 13

That afternoon, Lily sat in a wicker chair on the patio of her rented rooms near the clinic and gazed at the onion-shaped dome of the Russian convent across the lane. She couldn't adjust to the fact that Ari had returned and left again. *If he loves me, he would find a way to see me. If this relationship is one-sided . . . no, that can't be true.* "Wait for me," he said. *How long?*

To add to her confusion, she realized that on the very night that Ari returned to Bet Shalom, she'd dreamed she was inside the Russian convent looking for a key. The angel Michael appeared and told her to look outside in the garden. She woke before she found the key. Of course, she didn't reveal this dream to anyone. Dr. Klein might insist on more than outpatient therapy if she knew the visions were current.

As Lily sipped her coffee, a plan began to form haphazardly in her mind. *What did Michael tell me to do? Look for a key? What key? A house key? The key to the House of David?* She laughed as she partially recalled old Hebrew day school lessons about King David. Because of her recent dream she felt the answer must be somewhere in the convent.

How can I get inside? I've seen the Russian nuns buying milk and bread in the village grocery, like everyone else in Ain Karem. Other than that useless bit of knowledge, I know nothing about them. I'll pay them a social call. Neighbor to neighbor.

Lily walked down the lane with vigorous strides. The lack of rain caused the dust to lie like fine cocoa powder on the cobblestones. She liked walking in leather sandals with the dry dust between her toes. With her shoulders back and her chest forward, she felt like an ancient Maccabean warrior. She looked at the terraced hillside and noticed the olives ready for harvesting, the green ones for pickling, the ripe black ones for crushing in the oil press.

At the convent gate she pulled the bell rope. After a long wait, the small door within the larger gate opened. A young nun, dressed in a black skirt and gray blouse with a yoked bodice, stared at her with pale blue eyes.

"I want to see the Mother Superior," Lily said in a voice that sounded more confident than she felt.

The nun nodded, indicating she understood English, and motioned for Lily to follow her. A jungle of vines grew over the entrance, blocking the sunlight. Faint beams of light penetrated through the foliage here and there, casting a leafy pattern on the cobblestones. They entered a dark hallway with doors opening to the right and left. The nun pointed to the first door on the right. It led to a gloomy sitting room furnished in heavy mahogany furniture covered in wine red velvet.

"I will bring the Mother Superior," she said and abruptly left.

Lily was about to sit down when an elderly woman entered the room. She wore a black habit and tight-fitting head piece that revealed the outline of her bony skull.

"I am Sister Agnes. What can I do for you?" She said in English with a heavy Russian accent. Her head came only to Lily's shoulder, but her piercing eyes commanded attention.

Lily stepped back, intimidated. "I live across the lane. I can see your chapel from my terrace," Lily mumbled.

Sister Agnes' thin lips curved in a semblance of a smile. Her face, as wrinkled and dry as parchment, revealed nothing as she gazed at her visitor.

Lily stammered, momentarily at loss for words. *Should I tell her that an archangel ordered me to come here?* Before she could make up her mind, the nun began to speak in a delicate whisper.

"I refused to move to the Mount of Olives when Moscow replaced the sisters here with their own people. These new nuns are KGB. But of course, you knew that."

Lily nodded, even though she did not know this.

"Our founder was a prophetess with many visions." The nun looked at Lily with a curious gleam in her eyes.

"Yes?" Lily's confusion changed to curiosity at the mention of visions. Lily felt there was more the old nun wanted to tell her, but not in the presence of the younger nun who had just entered the room and positioned herself beside the settee.

"Would you like a tour of the garden?" Sister Agnes asked.

"Why not?" Lily replied, hoping for a chance to be alone with the elderly nun.

The young nun with the steel blue eyes stepped forward and offered to show Lily around.

To Lily's keen disappointment, Sister Agnes acquiesced.

"I must get back to my duties." She said and left the room without another word.

Lily followed her guide outside. The bright sunlight caused her to blink and rub her eyes. They followed a narrow path lined with small white stones. Lily noted the small cottages scattered amongst the trees and remarked on it.

"We live as contemplatives in individual hermitages," the nun curtly replied.

The path twisted and turned through a small forest of fir trees. On the other side, Lily noticed what appeared to be an abandoned rose garden. Clouds drifted across the sun, casting them temporarily in shadow. Then a cold breeze, which felt as if it came from the distant snow-capped peaks of Mt. Hermon, lifted Lily's hair in little swirls. Her heart raced as she felt energy pulsing up from the earth. She looked at the nun to see if she also felt something out of the ordinary. Maybe an earthquake?

The nun shook her head as if ridding it of cobwebs. Then she coldly told Lily that the visit was over.

Lily felt cheated. Something more should have happened, but she wasn't sure what. In any event, this dour Russian nun wanted her to leave the property at once.

That night Lily dreamed again about the archangel Michael. Just as she had described to Dr. Klein, his robe billowed out like a cloud, yet was a part of him. His eyes sparkled like diamonds. For the first time she noticed his feet. They were the color of her topaz ring.

There was something different about his voice. In her bedroom in Far Rockaway, he spoke softly, just above a whisper. Now, his voice bounced off the stone walls of her room, making her head ache. But his message was clear: She must return to the rose garden in the convent.

He disappeared as abruptly as he had appeared, leaving her awed and strangely energized.

At first light, Lily silently let herself into the front gate of Bet Shalom without a key. Like all the patients, she knew how to manipulate the latch with ease. She walked through the woods until she was in dense underbrush. Then she crawled on her hands and knees through the thicket until she came to a barbed-wire fence separating the clinic from the convent. Lying on her back, she inched her body under the lowest wire. On the other side of the fence, she crawled another three meters then stood and brushed the dirt and twigs out of her hair and off her clothes.

It took less than twenty minutes to find the rose garden. The unpruned rose bushes grew in gnarled confusion. Thorny undergrowth ripped her pants as she searched for some clue. She tore at the vines and weeds with her bare hands until she partially uncovered a marble statue of the Virgin Mary.

This tells me zip. Convents probably have dozens of these. Why did they bury and forget this one? I thought nuns pray and leave flowers before the Virgin. Lily shrugged. What does a Jewish girl know?

She sat on a flat stone matted with dirt and vegetation and looked at the statue in frustration. Absently, her fingers picked at the light green lichen on the stone beneath her. Then her fingertips felt smooth stone. Curious, she knelt and scraped off an area the size of a dinner plate and discovered ancient Hebrew letters carved in the basalt.

Her breath came in little bursts as she tore at the vegetation, not stopping until she cleared one entire surface of the black stone. Her finger tips bled now but she didn't care.

She found a piece of paper in her pocket, an old prescription for Valium that she never used, and a stub of a pencil. With these crude tools, it didn't take her long to make a pencil rubbing of the inscription.

Chapter 14

The next morning, Lily boarded the number twenty-seven bus in Ain Karem and rode to its last stop at Damascus Gate.

She walked down the middle of the crowded sidewalk toward the Mount of Olives, trying to mingle with buyers and sellers at the sheep market on the northern corner of the walled city. Wearing her paisley skirt and sandals, she looked out of place among the black-robed men in their red-and-white kaffiyehs and the women wearing embroidered tunics and gauzy, white head coverings. Fat-tailed sheep trotted down the ramps of small pickup trucks, and the smell of sheep dung and hashish accosted her nostrils.

Bedouin women presided over baskets of fresh figs sheltered from the glaring sun by the shade of the ancient walls. On any other day, Lily would buy some. Today her sense of mission propelled her on. She headed straight to the Rockefeller Museum on the corner opposite the Old City, weaving across the street between the traffic with not quite as much skill as the locals.

She paid the six-shekel entrance fee and strode up the stairs to the curator's office on the second floor. The building had the comfortingly familiar smell of a musty old library.

"I wish to speak to the curator," Lily said as she closed the door behind her.

"He's not in," said a young red-haired receptionist without looking up from her magazine.

Lily had enough experience with Israeli bureaucracy not to be deterred by a negative response.

"I'll see for myself." She crossed the room and opened an office door that read "Shlomo Aloni, Curator" in bold lettering.

Professor Aloni's hand stopped in mid-air, holding a match ready to light the pipe clenched between his teeth. He wore a white shirt with no tie and his collar open at the throat.

Lily smiled. "Your secretary told me to come in."

Looking mildly displeased, the professor laid down his pipe. "Please sit. Now, what can I do for you?"

Lily sat in a stiff-backed chair opposite the professor's desk. She introduced herself, but left out any mention of Bet Shalom. Then she unfolded the piece of paper with the pencil rubbings taken from the basalt stele in the rose garden.

"Can you translate it?" She handed him the slip of paper.

He put on his glasses and stared at the tracing. "This looks like ancient Hebrew. Where did you find this?"

"I'm not at liberty to say," she replied, primly crossing her legs.

"This is fascinating." He took a handkerchief out of his pocket and dabbed at the moisture on his bald scalp. "If this is authentic . . . this find could possibly eclipse the discovery of the Dead Sea Scrolls."

Lily felt heat rising in her cheeks as her excitement mounted. "What does it say?"

Aloni started to say something, shook his head, then adjusted his glasses. "I will need a few hours to study this carefully. Can you return after lunch?" He made no move to return the slip of paper.

Lily agreed to return. She heard the professor's voice speaking to someone on the telephone before the office door closed.

Back at the sheep market, she watched the selling of mutton on the hoof. A stout matron, sitting against the wall, held up a piece of hand-embroidered cloth for her to consider.

"*Comma zeh*, how much?" Lily inquired.

"*Mea*, one hundred shekels."

Lily countered with half that amount.

"*Quais*, fine," the seller replied and handed her the cloth.

Because the transaction happened so quickly, she figured she paid too much. To make up for this, she determined to buy lunch as cheaply as possible.

Inside Herod's Gate, she passed a small cafe catering to Arab workmen and students from the Hebrew University at nearby Mount Scopes. The sign hanging precariously above the door proclaimed, in Arabic and English, "Uncle Mustache's Cafe."

She took a seat at a table near the fly-specked window. A waiter took her order and gave it to a cook with a handlebar mustache.

The grilled chicken and French fries tasted surprisingly good. The plate of boiled fava beans tasted even better. Lily ate with gusto, then wiped the grease off her fingers and returned to the Rockefeller. This time the secretary told her to go in.

Professor Aloni sat behind his desk with two books opened before him. "If this is authentic...." He paused and narrowed his eyes.

He's stalling, Lily thought. "Just read it to me."

Aloni cleared his throat and read in a low voice:

> "*In the End of Days, the Most High, the Holy One, commands the House of Israel to wait for the appearing of Melchi Zedek, the King of Salem.*"

He took off his glasses and leaned forward in his chair. "By the style of writing, I would venture a guess of approximately nine hundred BCE. Of course, I would have to examine the original to be positive."

Lily did not intend to reveal the whereabouts of the original stele. She thanked the professor for his time and stood. "I'll get in touch with you when I know more about what I'm supposed to do with this."

Aloni also stood and raised his palm open in supplication. "Don't leave," he pleaded.

Lily reluctantly sat down again.

"I need to know if you found this stone *in situ*?"

"What?" Lily frowned in confusion.

"In its original place, buried, or above ground? Or did you, for example, buy it in a shop or from a Bedouin shepherd?"

"Why is that important?" she asked.

"It matters a great deal. If you found the stone in situ there will likely be other artifacts that could authenticate the inscription."

"I understand." Lily frowned while she considered the ramifications of revealing the location of the stone to this man. She pictured a team of archaeologists frantically digging up the old rose garden at the convent.

"I need time to sort this out." Lily again stood to leave. "I'll keep in touch," she said and left Dr. Aloni's office.

As she passed the secretary's desk, she heard him call out, "At least leave your address and phone number."

Lily smiled and continued out the door. She had no intention of returning.

Chapter 15

Boris Criminski, Archimandrite of the Russian Church in Jerusalem, received an unwelcome visit from his superior. Sweat beaded on Boris's broad forehead and dampened the armpits of his heavy woolen robe as he chain smoked and drank vodka with his grim-faced visitor.

"Your only duty, Comrade Boris, is to maintain a semblance of normalcy to the operation here. What could be difficult about keeping a group of nuns in line?" The visitor, dressed in an expensive hand-tailored gray suit, enunciated each word in a manner intended to intimidate.

Boris mopped his damp face with a linen handkerchief then poured more vodka for his guest. He knew his position was sought after within the ranks of the Russian foreign service. With the post came a chauffeur-driven Mercedes and a home that seemed a palace by current Moscow standards. He was free to do as he pleased as long as he kept up a show of religiosity as required in the Holy City.

"But I visit the convent in Ain Karem at least once a week. The Mother Superior has never indicated any activity out of the ordinary." Boris frantically searched his memory.

"You've been living in this palace too long, Boris," the visitor said with unfeigned contempt. His pale blue eyes took in the heavy damask draperies and oriental carpets. "Ain Karem is thick with foreign agents. We know the convent phones are tapped, and we're picking up traces of electronic eavesdropping from the clinic next door."

"What makes you think that?" Boris's head ached as he anticipated the threat of transfer back to Moscow.

"The Israelis are watching who comes and goes at the convent. I can see by your expression that you are not aware of this."

Boris knew better than to give an honest reply. Admitting he knew nothing would hasten his departure. He silently debated his options, then replied, "We have nothing to fear from them. It's one of our own who is betraying us."

The visitor's eyelids lowered a fraction as he blew smoke upward. "Who are you suggesting? Surely, you're not accusing me?"

"No, not you. That old crone, Sister Agnes, the one who calls herself the Mother Superior." Boris thought he could detect a sense of relief in his interrogator's demeanor. He knew how to play the game: point the finger at someone else. An agent suspected was immediately recalled to Moscow. Now, his superior might easily be the one sent home for allowing this nun to stay on past her time.

The visitor's mood appeared less adversarial when he stood up to leave. Boris walked him to his car in the cobblestone courtyard.

Boris knew Sister Agnes had refused to join her sisters on the Mount of Olives when Moscow replaced all the Russian Orthodox nuns in Ain Karem with their own people. The White Russian nuns wanted separation from the KGB-picked Red Russian nuns. It was inexplicable to him why Sister Agnes remained in her solitary hermitage among the rose gardens in Ain Karem.

The next morning, Boris told his driver to have the car ready to take him to Ain Karem. "Don't call to let them know we're coming. When we get there, I don't want you listening to jazz on the car radio. Get out and learn what you can about any recent visitors."

The afternoon traffic moved slowly as they approached Zion Square. The driver honked and accelerated aggressively as if he intuited his boss's inner turmoil. Speeding down the boulevard to the junction where the road to Ain Karem meets Mount Herzl, he made a right turn.

"Slow down!" Boris shouted at his driver. "We can't attract attention as we enter the village."

The driver frowned and eased his foot off the gas pedal. It was his habit to take the narrow winding road at full speed, careening around the curves without any thought of oncoming traffic.

They roared into the graveled area that served as a parking lot for the convent. Normally, the Archimandrite phoned ahead so that the nuns would have the heavy metal gates open. Today he got out of the back seat without a word to the driver and jerked the bell rope at the locked gate.

A young nun opened the gate. Boris detected no surprise in her eyes at seeing the unexpected visitors. In the formal manner prescribed between church clergy and nuns they greeted each other with a stiff half bow.

"Tell Sister Agnes I'm here," he said. The nun hurried ahead of him to the small hermitage near the chapel.

The Mother Superior received him in the convent's small guest room. She sat stiffly in a straight-back chair with her fragile wrists resting on the wooden arms. Boris could see only the oval of her finely lined face and thin hands with enlarged veins.

"Your Eminence, we weren't expecting you today," she said without warmth.

Boris made the necessary polite inquiry into the health of the elderly nun. He drank a glass of strong tea with fresh mint, though he preferred his tea with lemon, then began his interrogation.

Sister Agnes answered his questions without fear, as he had known she would. What could he threaten her with? Death? Exile? Her long life was near its end and she knew it. Like a faithful family retainer, she had maintained her vigil at the convent for more than sixty years.

"Once more, try to remember if you have seen any unusual activity in the area. Any suspicious visitors to the convent, perhaps?" He tried to jog her memory. "Occasional tourists show up, don't they? You give them a tour of the chapel?"

"No visitors," she said bluntly and looked into the Archimandrite's clear blue eyes without blinking. The visit ended with Boris stymied by the rigid courtesy of the Mother Superior.

On the way home, his driver informed him that Sister Agnes had recently received someone for tea. She is an out-patient at the psychiatric clinic next door. "An American."

"Only the Americans would use a mental clinic for cover," Boris said with disgust.

Chapter 16

The first day of the week, Dr. Klein received a telephone call from a Mossad agent who identified himself as Motti Pincus. After giving his credentials, he requested, demanded in her opinion, that she meet him that afternoon at Cafe Atara.

"Be there at three o'clock sharp. It is a matter of national security," Pincus said.

She agreed to the meeting, hoping the agent was a little man. At five feet, eleven inches tall, she knew her bulky figure and blunt personality never failed to intimidate short men.

At fifteen minutes to three, Dr. Klein's aging Renault rattled into Jerusalem. She wasted another ten minutes looking for a parking space on King George Boulevard. Sweating with the exertion, she maneuvered her car into a no-parking zone and walked one block to Cafe Atara on the pedestrian mall. Every table was occupied as she approached the outside patio. Without breaking stride, she smoothed her hair back from her face.

A thin man with a bushy red beard and curly hair to match stood up and waved a lanky arm in her direction.

"I'm Agent Pincus," he said without smiling.

"Pleased to meet you," Dr. Klein replied, disappointed that he was slightly taller than she.

He ordered two coffees.

"Add poppyseed cake to that order." She appraised him with her eyes. "What's your first name? I can't sit here and call you Agent Pincus."

"Call me Motti, if it makes you feel better." He sat with his back to the wall and his pale blue eyes swept the circumference of the patio at regular intervals.

"Nu? So, why are you buying me my favorite coffee cake?"

"You treated Ari Ben Chaim in your clinic last year." He vigorously stirred two packets of sugar into his coffee.

"Are you familiar with the Jerusalem Syndrome?" She was stalling for time. She could only guess at how much the Mossad already knew.

Motti Pincus reached in his jacket and took out a small notebook and pen. He held the pen tightly in his slender fingers. "Enlighten me."

"I located my clinic in Jerusalem for good reason. I have a background in diagnosis and treatment of religious hysteria."

Pincus wrote in small and meticulous penmanship while she continued.

"Jerusalem exerts powerful influences on susceptible people," she said in a pedantic tone. "Some Christian is always ready to blow up the Dome of the Rock to usher in the return of the Messiah. The police frequently subdue a Jewish tourist running naked through the streets claiming to be the prophet Jeremiah. Pilgrims find themselves overcome with fervor walking in the footsteps of Jesus. Most come to their senses the moment their plane leaves the ground."

"What's this got to do with Ari Ben Chaim?" Pincus looked up from his notebook with a slight smile, as if he knew he was getting the runaround.

"This has nothing to do with Ari. Under no circumstance

would I break a sacred oath and breach medical confidentiality. I'm just telling you my background."

"I have read his file." Pincus impatiently pointed his pen at the doctor. "Where is he now?"

A gust of wind swept by, sending hats and papers flying. Dr. Klein bent to retrieve her napkin, grateful for the opportunity to hide her expression. She must protect all her patients and particularly Ari.

"I haven't seen him since he left for India. Then, he disappeared at Ben Gurion. Of course you know all that."

"We know he left his kibbutz last week and traveled to Jerusalem to see you. We urgently need to talk to him."

"Why?"

"Can't tell you. National security."

Dr. Klein nodded, but she felt uneasy. The interests of the state were most likely not in Ari's best interest.

"I'm here to recruit Ari, that's all I can tell you."

Dr. Klein lit another cigarette, lowered her eyelids to narrow slits and blew the acrid smoke in the agent's direction. "I'm not saying I know where he is, but I could try to send a message to him."

"Tell him to meet me at the bar in the King David."

"When?"

"Erev Shabbat. That gives you five days to contact him."

"How will he recognize you?"

"He knows what I look like."

Dr. Klein looked at the agent's red hair and freckled skin and nodded.

Chapter 17

Ari and Motti Pincus left the bar at the King David Hotel after one drink and took a taxi as far as Barclay's Bank on Jaffa Road. Pincus paid the cab driver and led the way down a narrow side street. They stopped in front of a nondescript two-story building. Ari couldn't discern if it was an office building or an apartment house because he could see no sign or name plate.

The door opened from the inside and a porter nodded to Pincus, leading Ari to suspect a hidden surveillance camera. They entered a dimly lit hall and climbed the stairs to a second-floor office. The room contained four wooden chairs around a table. A sideboard held an automatic coffee pot and an old-fashioned samovar.

"Coffee? Tea?" Pincus politely inquired.

"You didn't speak kindly when you interrogated me on the Hermon," Ari said. "Now you need me, right?"

"I didn't believe your story then," Pincus replied.

Ari walked over to the sideboard and poured himself a cup of black coffee. "So what are the Syrians doing now that makes you so uptight?"

Pincus sat at the table and motioned Ari to follow. "Just hear me out," he asked.

"*Beseder*, all right," Ari replied between tight lips.

"We are today with respect to biological terrorism where we were nearly thirty years ago with respect to conventional terrorism."

"What's that got to do with me?"

"We are receiving reports that Iran is stockpiling anthrax, botulism toxin, and the like." The deep lines on Pincus' face revealed a continuous lack of sleep. "There has never been a major biological terrorist attack; therefore, you can appreciate, we have no track record for analysis. That's where you come into the picture." He flashed a thin smile.

"I'm your first link with such a group?" Random thoughts raced through his head. *The Mossad can't know my birth father is from Qom. I'm not the type to lead a double life as a secret agent. I want to get on with my life and marry Lily. Could this be my chance to avenge the deaths of my parents and Dr. Rosen?*

"You are the only one we can send in under cover. We're depending on you, Ari."

Ari remained silent, so Pincus continued. "If what you told us is true, Reza and his group think you're their messiah. How could you fail?"

Ari felt his life was spinning out of control. "What happens if they figure out I'm not the Mahdi?"

"Don't worry, we'll keep you safe. Someone from logistics will explain how we keep you covered. You will never be alone."

Ari did not feel reassured but indicated for Pincus to continue.

"Some biological agents have been used in the past. For example, Bulgarian agents assassinated Georgi Markov, a Bulgarian émigré and writer for the British Broadcast Center, by stabbing him in London with an umbrella-type weapon that contained ricin."

Ari winced. He stared at the floor as he pictured how Miss Queller, the British nurse, might have died. He wanted to ask Pincus if ricin caused instant death or if the victim died slowly in agony. All he did was shake his head from side to side.

"You want to say something?" Pincus looked up with an alert expression in his eyes as if he had just heard a silent alarm go off in the distance.

"No." Ari was more convinced than ever that malignant forces were orchestrating the recent events in his life, but the Mossad agent was the last person he could confide in.

"We know Iran does not yet have the capacity to deliver biological warheads. That specter is at least ten years away."

"So what's the urgency then?" Ari forced himself to put all thoughts of assassination out of his mind and concentrate on the issue at hand.

"We anticipate a narrower range of tactics," Pincus said, dropping his voice to a whisper.

"Like in a hijacking or hostage situation?"

"Biological weapons could be used in those situations, but there's little incentive for terrorists to do so. The projected death toll would be no higher than if conventional weapons were used."

Ari started to say something, then thought better of it.

"The most likely tactic," Pincus continued in his grim monologue, "will be to release anthrax spores or botulism toxin into the air as a biological aerosol." Pincus slowly got up and wearily poured himself a cup of coffee. "Since these agents are odorless, invisible, and tasteless, no one would know that a terrorist attack is under way."

"How could they physically do that?" Ari couldn't believe what he was hearing.

"Several ways." Pincus held up one hand and ticked off each finger as he explained. "Aerosol canisters with timing devices left in airports or air-conditioning ducts in buildings, or directly contaminating bulk food supplies. Since there are no reliable detection systems, terrorists will be able to strike any target they desire."

Ari rose and walked over to the one window in the room. Looking out the dingy glass he saw few pedestrians and almost no cars. It was late Friday night and Jerusalem was shut down for the Sabbath. His thoughts turned to Lily, and he pictured the candle he knew would be flickering in her window. Would she wait for him if once again he disappeared?

"It's too dangerous to go back to Damascus," Ari said, still facing the window.

"Your gut instincts are correct, Ari. We wouldn't send you back there. Never go back, always onward, is our motto." Pincus smiled. "No, my friend, we want to send you directly to the source. Tehran."

Ari flinched, this time visibly. *Tehran.* He rolled the word silently around his tongue. Up to this point he had been ready to refuse Pincus. They couldn't force him to go undercover against his will.

"I assure you, Ari, we're good at this. We'll get a message to Reza Najmabadi requesting him to meet you in Tehran. He'll think it comes from you, of course. Then we transport you secretly to Cyprus. Under your new identity as Yusef Haddad, Cypriot arms dealer, you fly to Tehran where Reza will meet you at the Royal Tehran Hilton. So far so good?"

"I get the picture," Ari said, without committing himself or revealing a certain eagerness to go to Tehran and settle the score with Reza. "But how do I convince Reza that I am now an Arab gun dealer?"

Pincus leaned forward, warming to the subject with obvious enthusiasm. "Khomeini doesn't want the real Mahdi to suddenly show up. After all, he is doing a good job without him. Reza knows this. He is more than willing to go along with your cover story. You just have to convince him that it is all for the good of the Brotherhood.

Ari exhaled deeply. Only one thing could persuade him to take on the challenge. Revenge. Yes, he would do as Pincus requested, but for his own reasons, not the Mossad's. This time he would not be a helpless captive. He would make Reza pay for his complicity in his parents' death.

"We have confidence in you. No other Israeli has escaped captivity in Damascus. You have more than a little *mazal*."

Ari squirmed in his chair at the unexpected praise. Was it luck? Or was he the biggest fool in history? "What about the contingency plans you spoke of earlier?"

"You will be briefed about possible safe houses in Iran."

"Possible safe houses?"

"They change, almost daily, but I assure you, one will be there if you need it."

Ever since the kidnapping at Ben Gurion, Ari felt like a sacrificial goat being offered up on someone else's altar. Reza and the Brotherhood in Damascus want him to be their messiah, and now Pincus thinks he can save Israel from biological warfare. Ari hesitated for a long moment. Though compelled more by revenge than duty, he finally accepted the mission.

"The future of Israel depends on you," Pincus said, almost as a prayer.

Chapter 18

Ari boarded the Iran Air flight in London dressed in the first custom-made suit he had ever owned; in fact, the only suit he had ever owned. He felt as if everyone knew he was an impostor. Yesterday he flew in from Cyprus under the name of Yusef Haddad and booked the next flight leaving for Tehran. He figured that Iran was a country that people were leaving, not going to, and anticipated a near-empty flight. He was wrong. The plane was filled with Iranians carrying big plastic shopping bags from London stores.

Ari sat next to a middle-aged man with snow-white hair. To Ari's relief his seatmate spoke no English. None of the women on the flight wore head scarves or veils, leading Ari to believe that Khomeini's strict control existed only inside the country.

Reza dealt with the import of weapons in his government job in Damascus. It should be no problem, then, for Reza to take him to the holy city of Qom. Pincus had assured him that access to the man in charge of Iran's weapons program was a sure thing for a certified arms dealer. Ari felt no detail of this mission was guaranteed. He knew next to nothing about Reza's personal life. Is he married? Does he have a family in Tehran? How responsible was Reza for the deaths of Moshe and Shifra? Could the Mossad keep him under surveillance? The unknown spun through his mind, making him dizzy.

He leaned back, stretched his legs, and pretended to sleep until they landed in Kuwait to refuel. No one left the plane there, and the steward served cool soft drinks saying that it was already 40 degrees centigrade outside the plane. He assured passengers that the temperature would be tolerable in Tehran.

Looking out the window as they flew over desert after desert, Ari did not know how it could be cooler where they were heading. But he had more on his mind than the weather. Layer upon layer of false or assumed identities lay heavy on his shoulders. First the *ben-meshak*, or kibbutz-raised teenager who loved to milk cows. Then the mental patient at Bet Shalom, or the first soldier in the history of the Israel Defense Force to lay down his weapon and refuse to serve. He fooled them in Damascus, pretending to be their long-awaited messiah. Even now he marveled at how quickly he had learned the Muslim prayer rituals.

Now, sitting on this plane in his expensive suit and a wallet full of British pounds, he felt almost comfortable as Yusef Haddad, arms dealer. Could he fool the Iranians? Before fear could take over his mind, he forced himself to look out the window and focus on the rapidly changing terrain shimmering in the distance.

The arrival terminal at the Tehran airport looked like a huge abandoned factory. Ari felt surprised by the grim facade. After the opulence of the Shah's regime he expected more. Even Ben Gurion Airport looked better than this dreary hall. He could see pale shadows on the walls where photographs of the Shah and his Shahbanou had been torn down and replaced with smaller revolutionary posters taped haphazardly in their place. The only color in the room was from the photos of Ayatollah Khomeini.

The customs clerk checked his papers and waved him through. Ari expected to be challenged on his identity papers, but the bored clerk took no interest in him. Bank Melli, Iran's Central Bank, had set up a few tables to exchange foreign currency.

Ari needed local money to pay the taxi driver, so he exchanged fifty English pounds. He did not have to wait for the delayed baggage carts. All he needed was in his one shoulder bag. Pincus had assured him that post-revolutionary Iran was not fashion conscious, and he would not need various changes of clothing.

His first impression of Tehran was disappointing. He felt as if he had stepped into a sepia-colored print, like switching from Technicolor to black-and-white. Everything looked washed out: faded brown buildings and streets, even the people wore gray or black clothing. He saw no nuances or shades of color. Israel had its deserts, but Tel Aviv or Jerusalem looked nothing like this.

The taxi drove first through south Tehran. It reminded him of Bombay, with its cramped dusty streets crowded with people. Continuing through the city, Ari saw the landscape gradually change. Soon they were on a tree-lined boulevard in north Tehran. They passed expensive apartment blocks and restaurants. He turned and looked back at what he thought must be an abandoned miniature golf course.

He asked the driver in English, "Did we just pass a miniature golf course?"

The driver shrugged. "Americans built that in the sixties."

From the airport to the leafy, shady boulevards of North Tehran, Ari saw slogans painted on walls in flowing Persian script. At a major intersection a traffic snarl held them up for over twenty minutes. The driver showed no concern.

Ari stared at two large posters plastered on the side of a building. They were obviously revolutionary posters. One showed a group of farmers plowing a field. The other showed a crowd raising rifles and machine guns as if in salute.

Ari asked his driver to translate the legend written in red paint above the posters.

It says, "The Twelfth Imam, we are waiting for you."

A chill settled in Ari's bones despite the heat of the afternoon. This was more than a people's revolution. Getting rid of the Shah and Savak, his hated secret police, had only been a means to an end. These people expected more. Was Khomeini it? Were they still waiting for the Mahdi, like Reza's group in Damascus? What would they do to him if they found out he was a Jew? Pincus had laughingly remarked that Muslims were circumcised too, so there was no danger in that department. What would Reza's group do if they found out he was working for the Mossad?

The taxi continued on a long, straight avenue with plane trees on either side. Their shade produced a welcomed respite from the glare of the sun. Just before they reached the foothills of the Alborz mountains, the taxi turned into the parking area of the Royal Tehran Hilton. Ari noticed the word royal had been painted over.

He paid the driver and entered the hotel. The lobby was nearly empty. The Hilton's French restaurant, Chez Maurice, looked like a bride jilted at the altar. Every table was laid with silver and linen, and adorned with fresh flowers, but only one table was occupied by a small family gathering.

At one end of the lobby, French doors led to a pool area. But only Westerners would swim in a public pool. The Westerners were long gone, and the pool lay empty and silent. On one wall was a poster of Yasser Arafat, of the Palestine Liberation Organization, wearing his perpetual five o'clock shadow, dark glasses, and the checkered red-and-white headdress. Ari smiled and almost felt at home until he saw the poster next to Arafat's. It depicted a veiled woman, seen from the back, lifting her child in her arms. There was blood running down her back, pooling in the road. Out of the blood on the road grew a red tulip representing the blood of martyrs. As he turned and took the elevator to his room, the hair on the back of Ari's neck stood up. He was not alone.

Ari slept fitfully in the luxurious bed. His back was more accustomed to a simple foam mattress on a wood frame. In the morning, the mountains north of Tehran appeared close enough to hike to, and Ari made a mental note of that as a possible escape route. By midday the peaks disappeared in the smog and haze hung over the city.

He needed more local currency than he'd bought in the airport. The desk clerk suggested he hire a taxi from the Hilton. The money changers, he assured Ari, would pay a better rate than the banks.

As he drove into the city he noticed details he had missed the previous day. The pot holes in the pavement looked old. Shop signs were dusty or broken. In the midst of a prosperous looking street, an abandoned building project looked just as the workers had left it, heaps of rubble blending into the scenery.

Cars and motorcycles careened through the streets in a pell-mell pattern, leading Ari to revise his belief that Israelis were the worst drivers in the world. A collision of a Fiat and an Iranian-made Peykan damaged only the fenders, but both drivers got out swinging. A crowd gathered immediately.

As the taxi picked up speed, pedestrians continued to move in and out of the traffic like bullfighters. They paused, advanced, gave way, dealt with each oncoming car in a graceful twist or turn. As far as Ari could see, his driver never even registered the pedestrians in his field of vision.

He found the money changers in little offices with plate glass windows that faced the walls of the British Embassy Compound. Each shop held one desk, two or three straight backed chairs, a telephone, iron safes, and a portrait of Khomeini. Ari chose one at random and quickly and efficiently changed five hundred pounds into toumans.

At a newspaper kiosk, Ari bought an English language magazine called *The Message of Peace*. He returned to the Hilton, tipped the driver well, and left a tip for the desk clerk who had earlier advised him where to find the money changers.

In his room, he propped himself up in the still unmade bed and read the magazine. He skipped through the articles that raged against the Great Satan—America—and its satellite—the Little Satan—Israel. As an Israeli he tended to ignore Muslim rhetoric. It caused him no alarm. Then an article on the biographies of the Shi'ite Imams caught his attention. Reza had seemed puzzled by his lack of knowledge in this area; he meant to rectify that lapse while he waited for Reza to show up. The Twelfth Imam was one of his secret identities, and he had to learn all he could about him.

Hearing a soft knock on the door, Ari walked silently to the door and peered through the peep hole. It was Reza, but his appearance had changed since Damascus. Ari warily unbolted the door and bid him come in. Reza hadn't shaved in days, and his clothes smelled as if they needed a good cleaning.

Ari controlled his urge to immediately confront Reza about his parents' deaths. There was much he wanted to know, but he couldn't show his hand now. To cover up his agitation, he called room service and ordered tea. "Include a bowl of fruit," he added after scrutinizing the black shadows rimming Reza's eyes. He hung up the phone and turned to his visitor. "You look bad."

"I've been followed night and day ever since I got your message." Reza sat on a chair, exhausted from the effort of talking.

Ari hoped the followers were his buddies in the Mossad. Pincus had said he would be under surveillance all the way.

A waiter in dingy whites delivered a silver tray with hot tea in little glasses. He also placed a plate of small pastries as well as a bowl of grapes and ripe peaches on the table. Ari thought this must be the last remnants of the royal treatment once given to the oil men who frequented the hotel in the past. The Hebrew verse, *Thou will prepare a table before me in the presence of mine enemy,* ran through Ari's mind. He smiled coldly at Reza.

Reza appeared to revive after two cups of *chai*. Then he became agitated when Ari told him he wanted to visit Qom.

"You wish to see your father's family? That would not be wise." Reza began to perspire. He pulled out a handkerchief and mopped his face.

Ari blanched at the mention of his birth father. Reza's response took him by surprise. He was in the persona of Yusef Haddad, arms dealer, and had momentarily forgotten that Reza related to him as the lost son of the Seyyed from Qom.

"You are right, of course. I have no desire to visit them at this time. There is more urgent business. I must see Ayatollah Zaheydeh," Ari said.

The anxiety lines on Reza's face now hardened into lines of fear. "That can be arranged, but may I ask your excellency why?"

"Zaheydeh is in charge of "unconventional warfare," Ari replied. *And I am in charge of bringing justice for my dead parents, he said silently.*

Chapter 19

Ari knew Qom was famous for the tomb of the sister of the Eighth Imam. He also knew that Khomeini once taught there before his exile to Baghdad. He wasn't making a hundred-mile trip through the desert to see Khomeini, though. The Mossad wanted him to contact a lesser known leader of the revolution who oversaw Iran's biological warfare complex, the Ayatollah Zaheydeh.

Reza set up the meeting between Yusef Haddad and the Ayatollah by hinting to Zaheydeh's personal secretary that Haddad could supply any weapon system they needed.

At the date and time arranged, Reza picked Ari up at the Hilton Hotel. They drove south and soon left the crowded city streets behind. An oil refinery polluted the air, then they were in true desert. There were no trees and the road dipped into valleys and climbed small ranges. From a small hilltop, Ari saw a salt lake that surprised him. He commented on it to Reza.

Reza answered in the dry monotone of a news broadcaster inured to catastrophe. "The Shah's secret police, Savak, dumped many bodies there. They tossed them out of helicopters, some dead, some still alive."

Ari made no reply but felt strangely relieved that the Shah was no longer in power.

To the left of the lake was a cemetery. "Martyrs of the Revolution are buried there," Reza added in the same flat tone.

In the distant background, the Tehran refinery belched smoke and flames in the air, giving the scene a hellish cast. The lake looked greenish in the middle, the edges fringed with white, cake-like salt.

Halfway to Qom, Reza pulled off the road and stopped at a cafe. "It's always better to eat before you get to Qom. You never know when they are fasting."

Reza ordered a rice dish with lentils and lamb meat. Ari ate a quarter of a ripe, pale green melon that tasted sweeter and crisper than watermelon.

They continued on to the holy city. Ari mentally pictured Qom looking like postcards he had seen of the magical city of Isfahan: blue domes, and sparkling minarets, men in brown silk robes and white turbans walking in silent meditation.

But Qom proved to be nothing like he had imagined. The city sprawled low in the desert surrounded by sheds, dingy buildings, and gas stations. The only object faintly resembling the architecture of Isfahan was the famous shrine with its gold dome.

Fear caused the muscles in Ari's back and neck to tighten. Yet Reza now seemed more relaxed, almost resigned, as they approached the center of the city.

They stopped near the mosque, where pilgrims rested in the shade, camping in the open cells along the courtyard. Whole families were taking their afternoon rest during the heat of the day. The peaceful scene should have calmed Ari's sense of impending danger, but it did not.

Reza got out of the car and walked over to a melon stall to ask directions to the home of Ayatollah Zaheydeh. The stallkeeper stirred from his nap and reluctantly pointed down the dusty street.

They drove a few blocks to a plain building made of yellow bricks. Ari could not tell if it was a residence, a school, or an army barracks. He hoped it wasn't the latter. A young man wearing a turban and gown, a rifle slung over his shoulder, checked their identity papers. He ushered them into his office where he made a brief phone call. Then they followed him through wide, tiled corridors to a spacious room covered in an assortment of fine, old carpets. The guide told them to take off their shoes and sit down. He stood beside them and proceeded to stare at them.

Three men entered and sat on the opposite side of the room. They wore black turbans and white, collarless tunics over two-button gowns of pale blue. Their thin black cotton cloaks looked like the gowns of medieval scholars.

Reza leaned over and whispered in Ari's ear, "They are students here for at least six years of theological studies."

"How many are there?" Ari asked.

"At least fifteen thousand."

"What do they study for six years?"

Reza replied, "They study logic, rhetoric, Islamic jurisprudence, philosophy, Arabic, and all its branches of grammar. There is no end to theological scholarship."

Ari thought of the Mea Sharim neighborhood in Jerusalem or Bnei Brak in Tel Aviv, where Orthodox Jews also made study their life's work. Communities devoted to Torah study.

Still, it was not the same. Muslim scholars and Jewish scholars were as different as oceans versus mountains, sweet versus savory. For the first time he began to understand the wide gap between himself and the Iranians.

A barefooted man with an Israeli-made submachine gun entered the room. Ari's pulse quickened. His hands felt clammy as he stared at the familiar weapon.

"He is coming. This is his bodyguard. Stand." Reza spoke in English for Ari's benefit.

Ayatollah Zaheydeh made a regal entrance, walking in measured strides. He was a small man with a narrow face. His mustache and beard, trimmed in a Van Dyke style, made him look as fierce as Ari expected. Under his thin black cloak he wore a two-button gown, like the students, only it was a light tan color, which made him look like a pheasant—only he was the hunter not the hunted.

The students awkwardly kissed his hand. Reza bowed from the waist and said, "It is good of you to receive us, though we be dust under your feet."

The Ayatollah dismissed the students with a subtle nod of his head and a lift of his eyebrow. The guard escorted them quickly out of the room before anyone sat down again.

They spent the next twenty minutes in pleasantries about the weather in Qom, the climate in Cyprus, and the good health of those present. Only after many rounds of tea had been consumed and the servant dismissed did Zaheydeh bring up the subject of Ari's visit to Qom, and then only in the most oblique terms.

Sweat dampened Ari's armpits. He wasn't prepared for the subtleties of oriental discourse. With effort he smothered his direct, if abrupt, Israeli way of getting to the point.

He tediously talked in generalities before asking his host what he needed in the way of advanced technology to further the advancement of the people's revolution.

The Ayatollah's prolonged answer on the economic needs of Iran made Ari regret his inattention during the briefing in

Jerusalem. Zaheydeh droned on about production costs and the price per barrel of crude oil in today's market. It finally dawned on Ari that this monologue was to soften him to accept the price they were willing to pay.

Several times, Ari looked in Reza's direction, hoping to catch his eye. Reza resolutely kept his eyes cast downward as he interpreted from Farsi to English and back again.

The Ayatollah stopped speaking just as Ari thought he could not stand the tension one minute longer. He sat there with a serene expression, incongruous with his wily features, and beamed at Ari.

Now what? How do I respond? Ari did the only thing he knew how to do. He put on his best poker face. He had always done well at cards. Evidently it was working because he could sense no overt hostility in the room.

Then the Ayatollah stood, murmuring something in low tones.

Reza simultaneously stood. With one hand he pulled on Ari's sleeve to indicate he should do the same.

Zaheydeh made his exit with no further ceremony. The guard escorted them outside to their car.

"You are approved." Reza spoke exuberantly in the privacy of the vehicle.

"What are you saying?" Privately, Ari marveled at the ease in which Reza had taken him to meet the Ayatollah. He knew Reza had connections, but he hadn't realized the magnitude until this moment.

"He has arranged to meet with you again at a secret military base near the Caspian. There you will receive the list of their military needs."

Ari swallowed with difficulty. He hadn't failed after all. They would provide what Motti Pincus called Iran's laundry list. This list would tell the Mossad more about what the Iranians didn't have than what they did have. Ari laughed with relief. He almost relaxed on the ride back to Tehran, but he observed Reza's grip on the steering wheel never slackened until they entered Tehran's outer suburbs.

"You didn't like being in Qom?" Ari asked.

"Why do you say that?" Reza's eyes glanced in the rear-view mirror.

"I felt you were afraid of being recognized," Ari replied.

"I was born in Qom. My mother still lives there."

Ari turned his head and looked intently at Reza. "Why didn't you take the time to go to visit her?"

"My mother is not well and is unable to receive visitors."

"You mean you couldn't visit her with me along."

Ari had hoped to meet Reza's mother. Not that he would consider harming her. Still, he wanted to see Reza suffer. It had something to do with being an orphan. He had been three years old when Moshe and Shifra took him out of the Baby Home in Jerusalem, so he had no memories of the years before his parents. Although on the kibbutz, he slept in the children's house rather than his parents' cottage, his adopted parents meant everything to him.

Now, driving through the desolate landscape between Qom and Tehran, he speculated on how his life might have been different if he had not been abandoned at birth. For the first time he acknowledged that being a foundling had significantly shaped his life. He sighed deeply, causing Reza to look at him out of the corner of his eye.

What a strange twist, him impersonating a Cypriot arms dealer. He had never told his recruiter in the Mossad that his birth father had been an Iranian from Qom. If they had known, they never would have sent him on this mission.

Feeling as if he was slipping into emotional quicksand, Ari changed the subject by asking Reza how he felt the meeting went with the Ayatollah.

"He has no idea who you really are. It must remain that way until we have all the controls in place," Reza said in an even tone.

You're right about that, friend. Even you have no clue who I really am, Ari thought.

It was midnight before Ari returned to his hotel. He asked Reza to let him out on the road. Under cover of the black, starless night, he circled around to the back and entered through a service door. Passing the sleeping front desk clerk, he took the stairway to his third floor room. He entered only after finding the silk thread he had placed across the door lock undisturbed and did not turn on a light until he was certain there was no unwelcome guest to greet him.

He called the front desk and ordered a late dinner, only to find the kitchen closed for the night. After a brief debate, the desk clerk agreed to send the bellboy to the kitchen to cook some eggs. When the meal was delivered to his room, he found the scrambled eggs cold, but the flat bread was tasty and warm.

Ari ate ravenously after the long day in the holy city. He felt pleased about how well the day had gone. If all went according to plan, he could get Zaheydeh's shopping list, deal with Reza, and be back in Israel within a fortnight. On that optimistic note, he decided to visit the gold bazaar in the morning and buy a ring for Lily.

Chapter 20

Lily slept fitfully, disturbed by the same dream that recurred in different forms. In the dream she was meeting Ari at the airport. Sometimes his body arrived in a coffin bound in a shroud. Other times, he wore a robe and turban like a Muslim holyman. In tonight's dream, he wore black military fatigues and carried an Uzi.

A sharp rap on her bedroom window startled her out of her nightmare. She glanced at the clock on the night stand—five minutes after midnight. *Who would come around at this hour? It's Ari. He's back.* She threw off the bedclothes and ran to open the door. "Ari?"

She gasped as if she had received a blow in the solar plexus. Staring at her in the dim moonlight was the wizened face of Sister Agnes.

"What are you doing here?" Lily's chest tightened and her breath came in short, harsh bursts so intense she had to sit down.

"I'm sorry I gave you a fright." Sister Agnes stepped inside and looked around the small sitting room. Then she walked to the adjoining kitchenette and filled a glass of water from the tap. "Drink this," she said, handing the glass to Lily.

Lily wheezed and coughed, then gratefully sipped the cool water.

Without being invited, Sister Agnes sat in a wicker chair and began to speak in a controlled but soft voice. "You are in danger and must leave Ain Karem. He intends to kill you."

"Who wants to kill me?" Lily felt faint. "Oh God, is the assassin back?"

"Assassin? Yes, Boris Criminski could be called that."

"Who?"

"The so-called Archimandrite." The nun spat out the word.

"But why?" Lily could feel the nun's distaste for the man, whoever he was.

"He's recently made inquiries about you."

"But he doesn't even know me."

"He knows you uncovered the black stone. Why else would he have interrogated me about my visitors. You are the only visitor I've had in months."

Lily started to say something, but Sister Agnes held up her bony finger and put it to her lips. "Do not speak. There is more. My time is over as guardian of the rose garden. I hoped to pass this task on to a younger sister, but that has not happened. You have been chosen to bear the burden."

"Wait a minute." Lily stood in protest.

"Hidden in underground caves below the rose garden are treasures from the House of David."

"No wonder Professor Aloni was excited. You probably have the ark of the covenant buried in your garden." Lily felt her overstrained nerves had her babbling about things she knew nothing about.

Sister Agnes stiffened at the mention of the ark. "You have told others?"

"Not exactly. I showed the curator of the Rockefeller Museum a pencil sketching of the stone stele. He doesn't know where I found it or where I live."

The wrinkles on the old woman's face deepened and she went pale.

"Can I get you a drink of water?" Lily feared the old nun might die in her sitting room.

"May God protect you," Sister Agnes muttered. "I have done all I can."

After the nun's departure, Lily felt emotionally drained. She flopped into an easy chair, pulled a soft afghan over her shoulders and tucked her legs up under her.

Sister Agnes is delusional in her old age. Maybe I'm the delusional one, dreaming about angels. Lily dozed, without dreams, in the comfort of the overstuffed chair.

She woke when sunlight splashed across her eyelids and stretched her long legs to relieve the cramped muscles. Sleep had returned clarity to her thinking. She now felt a compelling need to get out of Ain Karem. Away from the crazy nun and her buried treasures. Away from Bet Shalom. And she needed to be somewhere that didn't remind her of Ari.

Lily knew only one other person in Israel: Rachel, a friend from her hippie days in California. They had lost touch, neither one being much of a letter writer. But Lily remembered a postcard from Rachel. She lived in a little village called Rosh Pinna. Rachel had explained on the card that Rosh Pinna translated *head cornerstone*, a messianic reference of some sort.

Chapter 21

The sun had set by the time Lily reached Rosh Pinna, nestled on the lower slopes of Mount Gilboa. She got off the bus and walked up the center lane in the village, passing the homes of the original pioneers who had settled Rosh Pinna at the turn of the twentieth century. Just as the bus driver had explained, she found the ruins at the top, built of local fieldstone. Artists and hippies now lived in the restored homes.

"Do you know Rachel?" Lily asked a young boy who just came out of the ruins of a two-story house. She could see candles flickering in the windows of the basement.

"She owns the house with the blue door. Want me to take you there?"

The boy left her in front of the house. Lily stared at the blue door with yellow trim and noted the window frames painted a bright red. This place was not in a derelict condition like the house the boy lived in. Rachel had obviously spent money on restoration.

Lily lifted the antique silver knocker and rapped twice.

"*Ya voh*, come in."

Lily opened the door and walked into a large room, evidently the kitchen and living room. A woman in a long velvet tunic, no shoes, and a blue scarf stood at the stove stirring what smelled like spaghetti sauce.

Lily glanced up at strings of garlic and red peppers hanging from open beams. Deep in the rafters, she saw a sizable collection of spider webs.

"Rachel, it's me, Lily Towzer."

Rachel turned around, holding a big wooden spoon that dripped tomato sauce on the floor.

"Oh my God! Lily! What are you doing here?"

"I've been living in Jerusalem." Lily hesitated to say more.

Rachel put down the spoon and drained the spaghetti into a colander in the sink. Steam fogged up her glasses and she wiped them on her apron before looking long and hard at Lily.

"*Baruch haba*, welcome. Join me for supper."

The two ate spaghetti at a small kitchen table crowded with a wine bottle and jars of homemade pickles and olives. They finished off the bottle of wine as Lily brought Rachel up to date on recent events.

Rachel said little during Lily's monologue. At the conclusion she smiled then shrugged. "You're welcome to stay here as long as you like. I sleep upstairs in my studio. You can sleep on the sofa near the fireplace. It's cool at night so let the embers burn down slowly."

Lily found a musty eiderdown and two blankets on the back of the old sofa. She laid her head on a velvet throw pillow the color of amber wine and slept deeply without dreams.

Late the next morning, she woke and wandered around. She found toilet facilities off the back porch, obviously added to the original house. Her morning ablution accomplished, she went back into the house hoping to find Rachel awake and making coffee. She felt disappointment in finding the room empty. Walking upstairs she softly called out, "Anybody up yet?" When she received no answer, she gently pushed open the door to Rachel's studio.

The morning sun poured in from large dormer windows. Rachel stood before a partially completed tapestry. She was pinning pieces of colorful cloth together to create a vivid scene of Adam and Eve in *Gan Eden*.

"*Boker tov*, Lily. Now you see what I do. I *paint* pictures out of *schmattes*, bits and pieces of cloth pinned into place, then hand sown."

Lily glanced at completed tapestries leaning against the walls. Muted velvet flesh tones contrasted with lush satins and taffeta in brilliant shades of green, gold, and orange. Rough burlap overlapped with sheer muslin paisley. Pale blue cotton, the color of the Sea of Galilee at daybreak, blended with shimmery shades of faded silk shantung. What she saw impressed her, but she didn't know how to express her approval except to murmur, "I like it."

Lily breathed in deeply and slowly exhaled. "Maybe it's hearing a New York accent again, but I feel completely at home here."

Rachel laughed in a warm-hearted way that included everybody within hearing distance.

Chapter 22

Reza and Ari drove north, following a tortuous road over the Alborz mountains. They passed through isolated villages where simple huts clung to the sides of cliffs above raging rivers swollen with winter runoff.

Reza's plan was to rendezvous with the Ayatollah at a secret military base in the Caspian region. To accomplish this goal, they had to drive straight through without stopping for lodging.

"I don't want to drive this road after dark, and I definitely don't want to spend a cold night in a miserable, flea-infested guest house," Reza announced.

The back seat of Reza's borrowed Fiat held a round aluminum pot filled with pilaf and bundled in towels to keep the rice warm. There was also a flat loaf of bread, onions and tomatoes to be eaten whole, a jar of homemade pickles, and a crock of white goat cheese in salt water. He had not forgotten the samovar to make tea and a worn carpet to sit on. They sat silently by a stony river bed, drinking tea and eating their morning meal of bread and cheese.

In the bracing mountain air, where the only humans they saw were shepherds on distant ridges, Ari sensed Reza relaxing. For the first time since they met in the shrine on the Golan, he saw Reza smiling like a child as he took off his shoes and socks and waded among the rocks in the river bed.

As if in confirmation of Ari's intuition, Reza carefully dried his feet, put on his shoes and socks and said, "I haven't done that since I came here with my father as a child."

"I have good memories of fishing in the Jordan River with my father," Ari responded. He thought of Moshe teaching him how to attach hand-tied flies to the hook. Then he grew morose as he remembered how Moshe died. It would be simple to kill Reza here and throw his body in the river.

Reza stared at him with a strange expression that caused Ari to turn away. Packing up, they returned to the car in silence.

They stopped for the main meal of the day on a small plateau near the top of the mountain range. By noon Reza had grown anxious to get over the last high pass and start down the other side before dark, so anxious that he begged Ari's pardon and omitted the tea ritual after they ate the rice and lamb. They repacked the car hastily and set off on the last leg of their journey.

In the distance, Ari noted the zigzag trails that indicated the presence of wild mountain goats. It reminded him of the rocky strongholds above Ein Gedi, where herds of long-horned sheep and gazelle climbed the steep cliffs. He and the other recruits in boot camp had hiked in the Judean wilderness every chance they got.

The Fiat carrying Reza and Ari, straining in low gear, reached the top and began the long descent down the other side. The invigorating mountain air vanished, replaced by oppressive humidity. The rugged terrain changed so dramatically that Ari thought he had fallen asleep and was dreaming that he was back in India.

Jungles converged on either side of the country road. The luxuriant foliage revealed a spectrum of green. The air felt warm and balmy, and the humidity made beads of perspiration gather on Ari's upper lip. Where the farmers had cleared the land, Ari saw fields of rice paddies. He found it difficult to believe they were in the same country. Reza drove with his foot heavy on the gas pedal. Whatever light-hearted mood he had experienced in the mountains disappeared in the dank, muggy air of the Caspian region.

"How much farther?" Ari asked.

"Another hour. This secret military base used to be the Shah's winter palace and hunting grounds."

If Reza wondered why the Mahdi needed to make weapon deals with the Ayatollah, he was apparently astute enough to keep his queries to himself. Reza puzzled him in many other ways. He seemed like a man bent on doing his duty, fulfilling his obligation to the Brotherhood. Yet, Ari sensed inexplicable human affection from Reza, almost as if Reza regarded Ari as family. It made no sense, but then nothing had made sense since his abduction at Ben Gurion.

In the late afternoon they approached the wooden guard gate at the entrance to the old imperial hunting grounds. Reza left the car and showed their identity papers. The guard, a lanky youngster wearing a homemade uniform and carrying a Russian-made AK-47, called his superior on a radio phone for instructions.

With a cocky arrogance that came from youth and the overabundance of fire power, the guard pressed an electronic button that opened the gate. He motioned them through with a shrug of his left shoulder. Reza drove through the gate, mumbling curses on the young soldier's head for his surliness.

"Things will change when we're, I mean you're, in charge," Reza said by way of apology.

Ari nodded in what he hoped was an imperial manner. *How am I supposed to know how an Imam should act?* The weight of his supposed messianic status as the Holy One lay heavy on his shoulders. The charade was wearing thin. He reached down to pat his pocket. His trip to the bazaar earlier in the week had yielded just the right ring. He allowed himself a smile as he thought of putting the turquoise, surrounded by tiny diamonds, on Lily's finger.

The narrow lane became a deeply rutted dirt path. Once again Ari turned his attention to memorizing every detail of the terrain, knowing he would be required to draw maps from memory when he returned home. It was obvious that troop transports never took this road. Either there was another way in, with a paved road, or this base was so well hidden that it took few soldiers to guard it. This thought only served to increase his anxiety.

In the forest they came upon the palace, a three-story, circular mansion covered in pink stucco. Each floor supported a balcony with tall white pillars, making the whole structure look like a giant wedding cake. A bell-shaped turret crowned the top floor like a watch tower. Paint hung in strips from the upper balcony, and tattered awnings partially shielded the windows.

Reza parked in front of a marble pond more than forty feet across. A statue of a whale stood in the center, but no water spouted from its open mouth. Broad cement steps led up to the entrance, where a carved tiger appeared ready to pounce on visitors.

As they climbed, a robed cleric walked out the front door. He and Reza exchanged a profusion of flowery, archaic Persian greetings, each one declaring he was unworthy to wipe the dust from the other's venerable shoes. At precisely the same instant, the greeting stopped on both sides, and the mullah ushered them into the entrance hall.

The walls bore faded crimson tapestry, with flaking gilt trim on the moldings, a remnant of the late Shah's opulent lifestyle. Ari guessed the bare tile floors previously held rare and beautiful carpets. Their guide led them down the hall into a small antechamber where, at his bidding, they removed their shoes. Then they entered another room that had no furniture but three overlapping blue carpets.

Perspiration gathered in the small of Ari's back, soaking his waistband. One wrong word or gesture and he knew he would disappear in the regal ruins of this palace. The Mossad could not help him here.

Ari was expecting the Ayatollah Zaheydeh to walk in the room, with his mincing, partridge-like stride. Instead a man with military bearing, though in civilian clothes, officially greeted them. The man bowed in the old-fashioned, formal manner of the Persians.

"I am Colonel Melekzadeh, at your service." He spoke fluent English with only a trace of accent. "His honor, the Ayatollah Zaheydeh sends his greetings and regrets that he cannot be with us at this time. I am instructed to show you our facilities, after you have refreshed yourselves."

As he finished, a servant entered the room with a tray filled with steaming glasses of *chai*. Ari would have preferred a cold drink in the humid heat, but he followed Reza's example and sat cross-legged on the carpet to drink the tea.

Reza politely refused the plate of sweets offered and Ari did the same. Three times a servant offered the candied fruit and nuts and three times they refused. Ari wasn't sure what game Reza was playing but figured they had somehow made points by refusing to accept the dainties offered.

After a second round of tea, the Colonel stood and stiffly asked them to follow him. He took them through room after empty room, confirming Ari's suspicions that there were not many soldiers on duty here. One room had crayon drawings on the walls. He surmised that this had been the nursery for the Shah's young son, the boy who lost his inheritance when Khomeini took over the country. He wondered where the son was now. If alive, was he planning a counter coup? Would the son reopen diplomatic ties with Israel, as his late father had done? Ari had no time to speculate further.

The Colonel led them out a back door into a long neglected garden. They walked around a scummy fish pond choked with water lilies. Sunlight cast a sheen on the surface. They halted in front of a concrete bunker. *This reminds me of the bomb shelters at home. I actually liked it when the air-raid sirens sounded and forced us to go underground.*

As they entered the concrete bunker, the smell of stale air and mildew hit Ari's nostrils. This was a strangely comforting smell. *The kibbutz baby nurses saved their best stories and treats for those forays underground.*

Ari shook his head to clear away past memories. There would be no folk tales and sweets here. They followed Colonel Melekzadeh down the dirty steps into a concrete-lined room, six meters by ten meters. A bare light bulb hanging from the ceiling cast their faces in unflattering light but revealed nothing sinister in the room.

The Colonel raised his hand, as if in signal, and a hidden door opened to Ari's right. They went down a corridor fifteen paces, which Ari silently counted, memorizing each detail in the event they tried to keep him here against his will. He remembered Motti Pincus' final words of advice: "Always devise your own escape plan. We'll keep you covered, but just in case." Now that bit of advice seemed even more important.

They entered a door that led into a large room paneled in teak wood, where the Shah and his family must have intended to wait out an attack on the hunting palace.

From this luxuriously appointed room they went into an adjoining warren of cubicles that had obviously been added as research laboratories.

"All are equipped with safety hoods and air purification systems installed by Russian scientists," the Colonel said smugly.

A pale chemist wearing a dirty white lab coat looked up, then put down the flask from which he was pouring a yellow liquid into vials.

Reza hesitated at the door to the cubicle, afraid to go farther. "Is it safe for us to enter?"

"All biological agents are kept in another room under special refrigeration," the man in the lab coat said. Then he gave them a quick explanation of his work.

Ari wanted to question the Russian, but the Colonel took Ari's elbow and led him back through the bomb shelter, then up to a derelict gazebo in the garden. The cloying smell of honeysuckle hung in the air as they sat on rain-weathered benches. The place had the air of faded glory and decline. Compared to the modern military complex in Dimona, which contained Israel's nuclear capabilities, this place appeared deceptively benign.

"There are other biological warfare laboratories scattered across the country," said the Colonel. "Supplied by Russia. The problem is the delivery system. Our Air Force does not have missile technology capable of hitting targets as far away as Tel Aviv."

"You want to buy rockets that can deliver a payload to the Little Satan, Israel?" Reza asked politely.

"Let me speak candidly," Ari said, controlling his diction and the cadence of his words, trying not to reveal the horror gripping his mind. "You know the Jews can and will retaliate with nuclear weapons?"

The Colonel permitted himself a hoarse laugh. "Russia is building us three nuclear reactors in Bushehr. More than a thousand Russian engineers and technicians work on the site and are expected to install the reactor's main turbine this month. We are sixty-five million people. Israel is less than six million. When it is all over who do you think will survive?"

Ari mentally recoiled at the implications of what he was hearing. Did the Mossad know about the nuclear installation in Bushehr? Cold sweat spread from his armpits and soaked his shirt. He realized his question had been foolish and he regretted asking it.

"*Qorban*, sacrifice is sweet as mothers' milk to a true Shi'ite," Colonel Melekzadeh replied.

Reza nodded in agreement, leaving Ari the lone man out in this discussion. Ari admitted to himself what he had suspected all along. These people were operating in a parallel universe. There was no common ground. Iran and Israel could never negotiate terms of engagement, or terms of surrender.

By the end of the day, he had received Iran's list of needed military equipment that would enable them to carry out their planned destruction of Israel and eventual leadership of the Middle East. Ari calmly assured the Colonel that he could supply most if not everything on the list. He was able to speak with authority because Motti Pincus had prepared him with a price list. It contained every conceivable weapon, missile launcher, and rocket base produced anywhere from the USA to North Korea.

The day ended over a dinner of chehlo kebab and rice served in the once opulent but now seedy dining room of the deposed Shah.

Reza and the Colonel wolfed down the rice and grilled meat with large tablespoons, hardly stopping to breathe. Ari, appalled at the bleak future Iran planned for Israel, picked at his plate of rice, shoving the grilled lamb under the yogurt salad. He felt an emptiness in the pit of his stomach that food could not satisfy.

"Something is wrong with your meal?" Reza asked.

Ari patted his stomach and admitted some minor intestinal distress. He wasn't faking that. The river water he drank in the mountains was having its effect on his system.

"Please excuse me," Ari said and went into the garden to find the outhouse. He had noticed the palace was equipped with modern bathrooms, even bidets, but he saw that the piped water system had long since broken down. Only the underground laboratories were kept in prime condition.

Squatting over a cement hole in the outhouse, Ari stared at a two-inch cockroach sitting behind the water can and wished he were back in Israel. Motti Pincus would have told Dr. Klein that he had sent Ari on an urgent mission. She in turn would have informed Lily. Would she wait for him?

A sharp spasm in his guts caused him to grimace. He gritted his teeth, determined to get on with his life, as Ari Ben Chaim—not the Imam, and not Yusef Haddad.

He spent a fitful, sleepless night under a mosquito net on a narrow bed. The next morning he and Reza hardly spoke on the journey back to Tehran.

Chapter 23

The shrill, insistent shriek of the phone woke Ari out of a deep, dreamless sleep. He looked at his watch. Who would call in the middle of the night? He sat up, his heart pounding in fear as he reluctantly picked up the receiver.

A woman speaking in heavily accented English said, "Reza's life is in danger, meet him at the abandoned mini golf." She hung up before Ari could respond.

A vague mental image came to his mind. Hadn't he commented on the presence of a miniature golf course to the taxi driver? He dressed in less than a minute and raced down the stairwell that led to the service entrance of the hotel. Confident that no one saw him, he slipped into the dark shadows. The mini golf was at least three miles away, but the deserted road slanted downward and he made good time.

As the moon moved out from behind the clouds, Ari caught a glimpse of the restaurant next to the golf course. All the windows appeared haphazardly boarded up, as if the owner had left in a hurry. He deliberately avoided the entrance and circled around to the back.

"It's me," a voice whispered.

Ari froze, then slowly turned to the source of the voice. He slipped his dagger from its ankle strap and automatically went into a defensive crouch. "Reza?"

"I have a car waiting on the other side. Follow me," Reza hissed.

They wound their way through the ruins of toy bridges, castles, and putting greens. Ari saw the outline of a black sedan with the motor running but the lights out. Reza opened the back door and they both got in. The vehicle drove off into the night with no headlights. The driver wore a black hood.

"Someone you know, I hope." Ari's voice tightened with tension.

Reza gave a low laugh. "My sister, Ferideh."

Ari looked into the rearview mirror at a pair of khol-painted eyes that were neither friendly nor hostile. He swallowed hard. Meeting Reza's sister would only make it more difficult to kill him. This business of vengeance was turning out to be much harder than he imagined.

"I am the one who called you at your hotel."

"Where are you taking me?"

"Someone betrayed us in Qom. They know we are with the Brotherhood."

"What will you do now?" Ari asked. Motti Pincus had drilled him about the intricacies of the Shi'ites internecine battles. He knew Abd Umar's group in Damascus posed a threat to the stability of Khomeini's regime.

Reza ignored Ari's question and continued in his own train of thought. "I introduced you in Qom as Yusef Haddad, a Cypriot arms dealer, as you requested. Now I must go underground as well as this man called Haddad. My sister is taking us to a property in Karaj, where our family owns a small summer house. I will hide there until I slip out of the country with false papers. Yusef Haddad will cease to exist. You must do what you have to do, Your Excellency."

By using the honorific title, Ari knew that Reza was once again relating to him as the Hidden Imam, with powers of occultation. Reza expected him to appear and disappear at will. He would indeed disappear, as soon as he found the safe house provided by the Mossad. But not before he avenged his parents' violent deaths. He admitted to himself that it would be harder now that he met Reza's sister.

Shortly after dawn, the sedan drove down a dirt lane and stopped before a mud brick wall. Reza got out and opened the wooden gate, and Ferideh drove in. Ari saw a small, flat-roofed house with a large verandah. The rest of the property contained a peach orchard and vegetable garden.

An old woman, bent over with age, greeted them at the door. "This is Badri, the wife of the caretaker." Reza's voice revealed obvious affection for the old woman.

"This house is made of handmade, clay bricks. My father had it built fifty years ago," said Reza. "In its time, it was considered spacious and innovative because of the brick oven and grill in the kitchen. It even has its own bathhouse, or *hamam*."

A curious mixture of smells simultaneously enticed and repelled Ari. The sweet fragrance of peach blossom drifted in from the garden. In the kitchen the smell of kerosene fought to overwhelm the aroma of onions and garlic frying in a type of oil that was unknown to Ari.

"What's she cooking with?" Ari asked, involuntarily wrinkling his nose.

"Sheep's fat," Reza replied. "Only Persian sheep have these large, flat tails full of perfumed fat. Badri Khanum is already preparing our lunch. She keeps this place clean with no modern appliances and cooks on two kerosene burners. After her predawn prayers and a glass of hot tea, she begins right away to prepare the midday *khroush*, stew."

Ari nervously scanned the kitchen looking for a possible escape route. He knew they would come looking for Reza when they didn't find him in Tehran. "Don't you think the Ayatollah's men will find you here?"

"We have maybe one day of respite. Let me show you what my father secretly built."

He pulled back a curtain and walked into the pantry filled with sacks of rice, crocks of tomato paste, and jars of salted cucumbers. A large wooden wardrobe stood against the wall at the end of the narrow room.

"Here, help me move this," Reza said, indicating the wardrobe.

Ari thought it would take his and Reza's combined strength to move it out from the wall, but he was wrong. They easily pushed it aside. There was just enough room for a grown man to slip into a hidden space behind the pantry. Ari saw no windows, but the air felt fresh so apparently it had ventilation.

"When they come, I will be hiding here." He picked up a metal bar embedded in the cement floor and a rounded hook on the other end. He inserted the hook into a device on the back of the wardrobe and Ari could see that no one would be able to move the wardrobe from the other side.

"And your sister?" Ari asked. "Will she hide here also?"

"No, she will return to her husband's home today. But if necessary she is willing to sacrifice her life."

Ari felt the blood rush to his head as his outrage mounted. How many innocent souls would have to die for this crazy scheme? Without thinking, he shouted out, "No! She doesn't have to die."

Reza stared at Ari in the strange way he had often done before. A smile appeared on his lips then moved up to lighten his eyes. He knelt down and kissed the top of Ari's dusty shoes, then stood and put his hand over his heart. "You are most compassionate and powerful. I should have known you would not allow them to kill your own sister, your blood kin."

Ari's heart skipped a beat. The air in the little chamber felt oppressive, as if it was crushing the life out of him. He saw Reza's lips moving but could hear nothing. His mind refused to accept these unwanted revelations.

Reza gently put his arm around Ari's shoulder and led him back into the kitchen.

Ferideh, without her black veil, but her hair still covered in a white scarf, was pouring tea. She looked up at her brother with a worried expression.

"I have told him, dear. You will not have to sacrifice your life. He knows we three are children of the same father."

Chapter 24

Behind Rachel's house was a wadi, a wide, deep ravine filled with graceful oak trees, where Lily gathered wild mushrooms that smelled musty and slightly briny, like the sea. She also picked a handful of anemones, lupine, and red poppies. Then she found a small stream and took off her sandals to wade in the water, letting the mud squish between her toes.

She wandered slowly up the wadi and discovered an abandoned village of crumbling stone houses. The ghost village made her feel uncomfortable, as if she were trespassing in a graveyard, so she turned back.

She found Rachel in a back room sorting through piles of remnants: silk, brocade, velvet, sateen, cotton, linen, taffeta, lace. Rachel straightened and put her hand to the small of her back. "Time for a break."

Over cups of a tea made from the fragrant lemongrass growing in a metal can on the balcony, Lily asked Rachel about the ruins in the wadi.

"Arabs lived there. In 1948, they gathered their belongings, walked down the hillside, then crossed the Jordan River."

"Was it so easy to enter Jordan?" Lily thought of the difficulty that tourists now faced when trying to cross into Jordan at the Allenby Bridge. She had tried making a day trip to Amman.

The Israelis let her cross the bridge with her American passport. The soldiers on the Jordanian side of the river sent her back when they saw her Hebrew name.

Rachel snorted. "They were already Jordanian citizens. This was all a part of Jordan before, as you well know."

Lily didn't know. She knew almost nothing about the Palestinians. It was news to her that they held Jordanian passports.

"It was weird, like walking in a ghost town. All that remains are the foundation stones and a three-story structure with the rusted fire escape, looking like a derelict transplant from New York. What's a tenement doing in a ravine in the Upper Galilee anyway?" Lily asked.

"The story goes that a young man of the village went to Chicago and made good. He came back and built a modern apartment block. Of course, no one wanted to live in it even before they abandoned the village."

"How come people wouldn't live in his high-rise?"

"Arabs prefer a house with a courtyard and an individual garden. I do, too. Apartment blocks are like rabbit hutches."

"Why did they leave?" Lily felt sympathy for the displaced villagers, even though she knew that technically they were the enemy.

"They didn't have to leave. The Jews in Rosh Pinna didn't want their homes or fields. They already had more than they could cultivate."

"Why leave then? It's such a beautiful wadi." Frown lines furrowed her brow as she thought of what Ari went through while on active duty. She needed to know if atrocities occurred beneath the silent oak trees. Rachel's answer would determine if she ever went back there.

"The Arabs lost the war. If they had won, they would have looted the homes of the Jewish farmers in Rosh Pinna. They presumed the Jews would do the same to them. At least, their leaders made them think that."

"What happened to the man who went to Chicago and came back with modern ideas?" Lily could at least identify with someone trying to make a new start.

"I suppose he went back to America." Rachel pressed her lips in a tight line revealing how uncomfortable the subject made her feel. "I need to get back to my work."

Lily felt she had somehow offended Rachel with all her questions. To make amends, she asked Rachel to teach her to embroider. Rachel responded as Lily hoped she would. Lily learned quickly and, while Rachel pieced together the small scraps for a tapestry, she settled into a worn easy-chair and embroidered her first pillow cover from a design that Rachel drew on tracing paper. Lily thought that perhaps she could sell her work to the same dealer in Tel Aviv that handled Rachel's work.

After a few days, Lily felt the need to talk about Ari. He had never been far from her thoughts. His kibbutz was just ten kilometers down the main road. The temptation to visit there never left her, but an inner voice whispered, *Don't leave Rosh Pinna*. Instead she confided her longings to Rachel.

Her voice trembled when she first said his name out loud. "I'm in love. His name is Ari."

"Nu, so where is this man of yours?" Rachel asked, pragmatic as always.

"*Houtz l'eretz*, out of the country. I don't know where." Lily replied sadly.

"Ummmmm," Rachel murmured, a pin held firmly between her closed lips.

"We met at Bet Shalom."

Rachel lifted her head and laughed. "You met the love of your life in a crazy house? Tell me the whole story."

"Well, like I told you the first night, I was there because I was stupid enough to tell the immigration clerk at the Jewish Agency that I had communications with an archangel."

Rachel looked up from her sewing. "Do you really talk to angels?"

"Only in my dreams. You want to hear more?" Lily glanced at Rachel. Experience had taught her that not everybody wanted to hear her story.

"Continue, I'll let you know when I've had enough."

"Michael, the archangel, told me to come to Jerusalem. I came and ended up in Bet Shalom. Not a bad place." Lily's voice faltered.

"Go on," Rachel said.

"My psychiatrist was murdered. I don't want to talk about that."

"I understand," Rachel said quietly.

"His specialty was treating patients with the Jerusalem Syndrome."

"Is this the syndrome you were diagnosed with?" Rachel asked.

"No, that's what people with delusions have. I really heard and saw Michael."

"I believe in dreams," Rachel said as she laid her piecework down. "I studied the kabala and I know that the spiritual world exists. Most people tune it out, but I don't."

Encouraged by Rachel's attitude, Lily felt free to relate almost everything that had happened during her stay at Bet Shalom.

"What brought Ari there?" Rachel asked.

"You probably heard about him on the evening news. He was one of the four soldiers involved in the Abu Tur incident. You remember? Where the soldiers buried the Palestinian teenagers alive. But Ari refused to participate, and handed his gun to his C.O. After that, he had a nervous breakdown and his kibbutz sent him to Bet Shalom."

"I remember the incident. But none of the boys died. He shouldn't have blamed himself."

"The public never heard that Ari was an orphan, abandoned at birth. Turns out his father was an Arab."

"That's enough to give a kibbutznik a breakdown," replied Rachel.

A knock on the back door interrupted their conversation. A young woman with two small, tow-headed boys entered the room.

"Chantal. *Ahlan*, welcome. Meet Lily." Rachel laid her work down and put the teakettle on to boil for the visitors. "Do the boys want to drink tea?"

"They drink anything," Chantal said in English with a heavy French accent.

Rachel explained that Chantal, her husband, and children all camped in the wadi. "I'm surprised you didn't bump into them on your morning walks," she added.

"We're not in wadi in the morning. We go find food," Chantal explained. "We pick apricots and pecans."

"They live off the land, so to speak," Rachel said, putting a loaf of homemade bread and a jar of plum jam on the table. "Chantal's husband thinks this is the end times."

By the tone in Rachel's voice, Lily could tell she didn't approve of Chantal's husband. Lily didn't think it was because of his peculiar views. It probably had more to do with his not providing food and shelter for his family. Still, the words "end time" caused her pulse to increase as she thought about the inscription on the stone in the Russian convent: *Watch for Melchi Zedek, the King of Salem, who will appear in the End of Days.*

"What brought you to Israel?" Lily asked, more than a little curious.

"As you may have guessed by my accent, I am French." Chantal shrugged as if she had been asked this question often. "We came with our son, David. Emmanuel was born in Jerusalem. I gave birth in a youth hostel while Serge was looking for work. The owner of the hostel felt sorry for us and gave us the use of a house on the back side of the Mount of Olives. The house had furniture, even a refrigerator. I was happy there, but Serge came home one day and said we must leave everything and go to the desert. We left that night and wandered around. Ended up here."

"Life in the wadi hasn't dampened your spirit." Lily marveled at Chantal's beautiful complexion and the dark tan on the boys' bare legs.

"When the winter rains come," Rachel said, "they'll get sick, malaria, who knows what else. I'm urging Chantal to write home for airplane tickets." They finished their tea and bread in silence. Rachel swept the crumbs on to a dish towel and tossed them out the open window for the birds.

After Chantal and her boys left, Lily couldn't get the French family out of her thoughts. *Why would they wander around Israel believing it was the end times? Was this equivalent to speaking to angels? Am I like them?*

Lily decided now was the time to tell Rachel about the convent.

"Rachel, there's more to my story about Bet Shalom. Do you want to hear it?"

"Of course, *motek*, darling, you intrigue me."

"Michael instructed me to visit the Russian convent next door to the clinic."

"Are you sure it wasn't simply power of suggestion? Who wouldn't be curious about Russian nuns?" Rachel slipped the needle in and out of rose colored velvet.

"No, it was definitely on Michael's orders that I paid a visit to Sister Agnes. Later, in the convent garden, I found a black stone engraved with ancient Hebrew. I took a pencil etching of it to a Professor Aloni at the Rockefeller Museum."

Rachel stopped sewing, the needle pausing in mid-air. She looked at Lily with alert expectation. "Go on."

"He deciphered the inscription. Something about the *end of days*."

"Don't make any connection between what you're telling me now and what you just heard about Chantal's husband. He's a sicko, dragging his family around thinking it's the end times."

Lily wanted to believe Rachel. Yet some intuition, or premonition, she couldn't tell the difference anymore, told her that it wasn't merely a coincidence that she had come to Rosh Pinna. She reached in her pocket and pulled out a rumpled piece of paper and handed it to Rachel.

"What's this?"

"The inscription from the black stone. It's ancient Hebrew."

"Can you read it?" Rachel held the paper up to the light.

Lily sighed and shrugged her shoulders deeper into the chair. "My father was a furrier but he always dreamed of a life spent studying Torah. He kept a large collection of Judaica."

Rachel nodded knowingly. "Yeah, my dad also had a massive library. I inherited it." She pointed to the floor-to-ceiling bookcases chock full of old books.

Lily looked with envy at Rachel. "I never learned to read Hebrew. My father never let me touch his books. He wanted a son and he was disappointed when all he got was me. He would have sent a son to yeshiva and supported him throughout his life as a Talmudic scholar."

She had never made this admission to anyone, even to Dr. Klein. It felt good to freely reveal her outrage at her father and marveled that she hadn't done it sooner.

Rachel took a book off the shelf and blew the dust off. "I loved to play in my father's study, pulling books off the shelves to look at the engravings. By the age of six he had taught me the Hebrew alphabet."

"So why did you ever leave home? If my father had been like yours, I never would have left," Lily said.

Rachel laughed. "I wanted to travel to California with a bunch of hippies. That's how I met you! But you know me, always in search of the perfect commune. I came to Israel."

Rachel sneezed from the dust. "I've got a hunch. This find of yours could be bigger than anything you've ever dreamed of."

"That's saying a lot, considering I dream about angels," Lily replied.

Ignoring the sarcasm, Rachel put the open book on her lap and began to explain the various theories about the lost ark of the covenant.

"One theory is that the Queen of Sheba and King Solomon had a son. Sometime after Solomon's death, the Egyptian army conquered his kingdom. The story goes that this son, raised in the courts of Solomon, took the ark away before Sheshak, the head of the Egyptian forces, could capture it. In those days, people recognized the power of the ark. Ethiopians still believe it is safely hidden in a cathedral in Addis Ababa."

"Fat chance of that!" Lily responded emphatically. "Go on. I can tell there is more."

"OK. Another theory is that King Nebuchadnezzar carried the ark to Babylon after he burned Jerusalem around 600 BC. If that's true, then it's still buried somewhere in Iraq or southern Iran."

"Definitely out of reach then."

Rachel continued reading. "Certain rabbinical sources suggest the ark is buried in a secret cave on Mount Nebo, across the River Jordan. That corresponds to where Moses is said to be buried, but to this day no one has found his grave."

"I've heard the Vatican has the ark."

"I've heard that, too. After the razing of the second Temple in 70 AD, the Romans took the ark as booty and buried it in the vaults beneath what is now the Vatican. So deeply buried that no one can find it, even today."

"So which theory do you believe?" Lily asked.

"They're all seriously flawed. Don't you see it?" Rachel stood up and took another volume off the shelf. "I want you to hear a passage from the first book of Shmuel HaNavi, the Prophet Samuel. I have it in the English translation." Rachel read out loud the story of the Philistines capturing the ark of the covenant:

> *They placed the ark in their temple dedicated to the pagan god Dagon. When they returned the next morning, they found Dagon lying over the threshold with his arms broken. They put him back in place and when they returned the next morning, they found their god lying on the floor with his head broken off. Then their cities and villages were overrun with mice and all the people suffered painful hemorrhoids.*

"Look here," Rachel continued, laughing, "it says their cries went up to the heavens."

"You'd howl, too, if you had those things," Lily rejoined.

Rachel continued to read aloud about how the Philistine lords devised a plan to appease the god of the Hebrews by making an offering of golden mice and golden hemorrhoids. The Hebrews rejoiced at the return of the ark, but in their enthusiasm opened it and looked inside. Thirty-five thousand men of Israel died that day because they didn't have the anointing to touch the ark.

"There!" Rachel emphatically closed the book. "Do you see it? No one can possess it without suffering bad consequences. Later, when King David tried to bring the ark up to Jerusalem, one of his men reached out to steady it and he died on the spot."

"That's quite a story," Lily said, but I'm not looking to find the ark."

"The point I'm making," Rachel said patiently, "is that the ark can't be in Rome, or Addis Ababa or Iran or Iraq. If it were, they would be having plagues."

"What about Mount Nebo, where Moses is said to be buried?" Lily replied.

"That's a possibility. I can't think of a better resting place than with Moshe Rabinu's bones."

"So what's this to do with me?"

"Give me a minute." Rachel closed her eyes. It was so quiet in the room that Lily could hear the wind rustling in the top of the mulberry tree outside the window.

"Tell me exactly what's written on the stone monument in the Russian garden," Rachel said with her eyes still closed.

Lily recited from memory: *The Most High, the Holy One of Israel, commands the House of Israel to watch for Melchi Zedek, the King of Salem, who will appear in the End of Days.*

Rachel opened her eyes. "Let's take this one step at a time. Melchi Zedek translates king of righteousness. The king of Salem means king of Jerusalem."

"Could this be a reference to King David?" Lily asked.

"He was the only one whom God trusted with the power inherent in the ark, but let's leave King David out of this. Someone, perhaps a priest, buried the ark in a cave in Ain Karem."

"The only way to find out is to excavate the entire garden."

"That's impossible as long as the Russians live there, right?"

Chapter 25

Ari glanced at Ferideh in wonder mixed with pain, then, feeling embarrassed dropped his gaze. He had dreamed of this moment since his father had told him he was adopted. Now, conflicting emotions assailed his mind: joy at finding blood relatives, relief that his biological father wasn't a Palestinian, curiosity about his Persian siblings, and thinly veiled anger. Why were his Jewish parents murdered and these people not? Then his pragmatic Israeli nature forced him to face the present danger.

He took a deep breath and spoke in a firm voice. "I can't deal with this now. I've got to tell you something important, and we don't have much time." He put his palm up to stop Reza from interrupting him. "I may be your half-brother, but I am *not* the Twelfth Imam. I have no supernatural powers. I can't save you, and I must act fast to save myself."

Reza stood quietly and smiled. Ferideh looked anxiously at her older brother.

"You must believe me," Ari continued. "I'm an Israeli farmer. Fate seems to have arranged that we have the same biological father, but there is nothing more to it."

"What about this?" Reza's slender forefinger gently touched Ari's cheek.

Ari raised his hand and felt the small scar that had been there since birth. He had grown so accustomed to it that he nearly forgot it was there, even when shaving. The nurse at the Baby Home had named him Ari, the Hebrew word for lion, because of this birthmark. It proved nothing. But Ari saw in Reza's eyes that he could not be persuaded otherwise.

He recognized that Reza's plan to hide in the secret pantry was foolhardy. It would take the Ayatollah's men only minutes to force the family retainer to reveal all. They would take their chances with the safe house provided by the Mossad.

"Both of you, come with me," Ari said in his most commanding tone. "No time to explain. We have to get back to Tehran before the men from Qom pick up the trail."

Reza and Ferideh acquiesced with such speed, Ari wondered if that wasn't what they were planning all along. He insisted they send the servant woman away for her own protection. He looked on as they hugged the woman who had been their surrogate mother.

Ferideh opened her purse and gave Badri Khanum all her cash. Only then did they hurry to the black sedan. Reza sat behind the wheel with Ari in the passenger's seat. Ferideh, covered in a full-length chador, sat in the back. They waved goodbye, leaving a cloud of dust to settle on the old woman weeping in the gateway.

As they approached Tehran, Ari instructed Reza to go to the intersections of Talegani Boulevard and Avenue of the Revolution.

"On the corner you will see a Cinema house," he said, repeating instructions he had memorized in Jerusalem. "Go one block then take the first left turn. We should see a five-story building. Drive past it and go one short block and then turn right on a narrow lane."

Reza followed his directions and stopped in front of a one-story house with a high walled garden. The plaque on the door read *Madame Shirazi's Kindergarten*.

"Drive around the block again, I want to make sure we are not being followed," Ari said.

Reza did as he was told and made the difficult left turn into traffic, then turned left again on Talegani Boulevard. They passed the tall building and parked some distance from the house with the green door.

"Wait in the car while I make sure it's safe," Ari said.

His shoulders twitched as if he sensed unseen watchers. Nervously he pushed the door bell. After what seemed the longest twenty seconds in his life, the door opened a crack.

"*Bali?* Yes?" A middle-aged man peered out.

"Mordecai sent me," Ari said using the code word supplied by the Mossad. He thought his handlers in the Mossad could have thought of something more original than the name of Queen Esther's uncle.

The man opened the door wide enough to stick his head out and look up and down the street. He pulled his head in like a turtle in his shell when he saw the black sedan parked down the side street.

"They are with me," Ari said in rapid-fire Hebrew, at the same time shoving his foot in the doorway.

Openly unhappy, the man beckoned him to enter. Ari stood his ground and motioned to Reza and Ferideh to join him. When all three were inside, Ari introduced himself.

"I was told to expect only one," the man said in an aggrieved tone.

"Plans have changed. We can talk after you move the car." Ari reached for the keys in Reza's hands.

They walked into a sitting room with stiff-backed chairs lined up around the walls, like a mayor's office in a provincial small town. Two landscape paintings and a portrait of Khomeini adorned the walls at a level near the ceiling. Ari, taller than six feet, had to tilt his head back to view them. Reza and his sister sat in silence until their reluctant host returned, followed by a sallow-faced woman with a tray of tea in little glasses.

"You expect me to get all three of you out of the country?" the Mossad agent asked in terse Hebrew. "I cannot perform miracles."

Ari smiled at his newly found sister and brother. They smiled hesitantly back at him, somewhat confused that this man spoke Hebrew to the Mahdi. "Khomeini's people will kill them because they belong to an outlawed Brotherhood with headquarters in Damascus."

"What's that to do with us?" The agent took out a pack of Iranian cigarettes. "You smoke? Him?" He gestured at Reza. Only Ari accepted.

"I owe them a favor." Ari had no intention of telling this man they were his half brother and sister.

There was a long moment of silence. No sounds penetrated the thick walls of the building, and they could hear each other breathing.

"They will be looking for three people, so I must separate you."

Ari nodded. He had to trust this man to do the right thing for Reza and Ferideh.

The man continued in Hebrew. "I don't know how much they told you in Jerusalem, but not much I suspect. There are four ways out of Iran." He raised his thick fingers and ticked them off. "The Turkish border is the easiest." He inclined his head in Ferideh's direction.

"We can send one of you across the border with Pakistan, or via a barge to Oman from Bandar Abbas. The fourth route is via Azerbaijan. There are risks involved in each scenario, but perhaps the last one has the highest risk factor."

"Risk factor?" Ari already felt protective of his new found family and decided he would take the most dangerous route.

"Azerbaijan is on the border between Iran and Russia. Thanks to the American microwave stations sitting on the border, we can point you in the direction of a Russian station on the other side."

"That's good?" Ari's concern grew by the minute.

"After you cross the border, you will need to find a Russian patrol as quickly as possible. These mountains are full of hungry wolf packs."

"What about the Russians?"

"They won't send you back to Tehran, but you may have to spend some time in a Moscow jail before our boys can help you."

"And them?" Ari inclined his head a fraction of an inch toward Reza and Ferideh. They sat with their hands folded in their laps, their eyes fixed intently on Ari.

"Where do they want to go?" The Mossad agent asked as if he were a travel agent making arrangements for a holiday abroad.

Ari turned to Reza. "If they get you out of Iran, where do you want to go?"

"Ferideh will go to France. We have friends of the Brotherhood there. I must return to Damascus."

Ari's eyes narrowed at the mention of Damascus. Now he knew that Abd Umar was the man responsible for the murder of his parents, Dr. Rosen, and the nurse. Not Reza. Ari's fist clenched and released as he gave their destinations to the Mossad agent. The man stared hard at Ari, then left the room without speaking. He returned after ten minutes. "We can produce forged Iranian passports and exit visas for them, but they will have to travel as man and wife. It isn't possible for a woman to travel alone. They must leave tonight for the Turkish border."

Ari quickly translated from Hebrew to English and both Reza and Ferideh nodded in agreement.

"If I were in your shoes, I'd opt for the southern route. In either case, don't translate the details of your escape route in case they're captured," the agent said curtly.

Unannounced, the sallow-faced woman who had served them tea brought in a large round tray piled with saffron flavored rice and chicken. Ari ate hungrily. He noted with satisfaction that Reza and Ferideh ate with the same adrenaline-induced gusto. It might be a long time before they had a good meal, and it probably was the last meal they would eat together. He was sure Reza did not think so.

The brother and sister drove away in an old Peykan sedan before midnight. Reza and Ferideh wept and kissed his hands before getting into the car. Ari controlled his emotions, knowing the Mossad agent was watching. They were his only living relatives, and he never expected to see them again. If he got out of Iran alive, he would have to change his identity and live a hidden life as long as the Brotherhood considered him the Mahdi.

"Who do they think you are, the messiah?" the agent asked, a curious light in his eyes.

"Something like that," Ari replied, feeling blood rush to his head. His hand involuntarily moved to his face to cover the lion-shaped birthmark. Changing the subject he asked, "What happens to our car?"

The agent laughed, breaking the tension as the small sedan carrying his brother and sister drove out the gate with Ferideh waving to Ari through the back window. "It has already been dismantled into hundreds of spare parts that will find their way into the bazaar. We need to get you to Bandar Abbas."

"That's on the Strait of Hormuz, if I remember my maps correctly." Ari mentally readjusted to the urgent task at hand.

"Yes, just a short boat ride from Oman. You don't speak Farsi and that makes it difficult. You'd never pass the border inspection."

"What's your plan?" Ari felt anxious to get out of Tehran before sunup.

"You ride in a truck carrying a load of melons to Bandar Abbas. We know where the roadblocks are set up. The Army is too lazy to change their standard methods of operations. You can ride up front with the driver, and when necessary, you will hide under the melons."

Ari grimaced as he remembered the sickening ride from Ben Gurion Airport to Lebanon.

"You aren't up to it?" the agent asked.

"It sounds *joffe*, fine to me. What happens when I get to the port city?"

"We smuggle you across to Oman in a fisherman's dinghy. It's done every night by local smugglers. Once in Oman you will receive the necessary papers, a change of clothes, and you will take a plane out of Oman like a millionaire."

Ari knew the next twenty-four hours were critical, and his thoughts turned to Lily. Would he live to give her the ring? He ached to tell her he loved her.

Chapter 26

The comforting smell of fresh baked *challah* tickled Lily's nostrils as she drifted in and out of sleep. She lay listening to the faint sounds of her mother scrubbing the floor and shaking the rugs in preparation for the Sabbath. By the time Lily rose, washed and dressed, the kugel would be in the oven and the cholent simmering on the stove.

Then Lily turned over on the lumpy sofa, opened her eyes, and stared at the rafters. The array of silky, parachute-like cobwebs she saw there reminded her that she was in Rachel's living room in Rosh Pinna, not in her mother's immaculate home in Far Rockaway. She sat up, rubbed her eyes, and drew a breath. She realized she hadn't dreamed the odor of warm bread.

Lily slipped into a long denim skirt and a loose blouse and then padded barefoot to the kitchen to make herself a cup of coffee.

Rachel was bending over to remove a braided loaf from the oven. Without turning, Rachel explained, "I don't keep kosher, never go to shul, even on Yom Kippur, but every Friday, I bake two challah loafs and, just before sundown, I light a candle."

"That's fine by me," Lily responded. She didn't think Rachel owed her an explanation of her Sabbath preparations.

Rachel placed the hot pan on the counter, then turned to Lily. She cocked her head and eyed Lily with a quizzical expression.

"What? So I didn't brush my hair yet. Is it sticking up?" Lily patted her curly hair, embarrassed by the scrutiny.

"You look fine. I'm just thinking. I want you to meet some friends of mine. They live midway down the hill."

"Artists?" Lily asked.

"They call themselves *Messianic Jews*. I made this bread to take to their house tonight."

Lily shrugged, not feeling up to meeting new people. Messianics, Habadniks, Hassids, it was all the same to her. But she could see that Rachel expected her to go. "All right, I'll go, eat their chicken, drink their wine."

As the sun set behind Mount Gilboa it cast the village in purple twilight. A stray dog wandered down the lane, sniffing at each bush and cypress tree. The inhabitants of Rosh Pinna were settling down to enjoy their most elaborate meal of the week. Most families could afford chicken, a few bought beef or lamb.

Rachel and Lily stopped in front of a one-story stone house. "What kind of people live here? Artists or hippies?" Lily asked.

"They're like us. Sort of. You'll see." Rachel rang the bell and waited.

The door was opened by a handsome man with curly black hair that reminded Lily of Ari's. He greeted Rachel with a kiss on each cheek. Rachel introduced Lily, who stepped back in case he intended to greet her in the same way. Instead, he offered her a firm handshake, then led them through an entrance hall, a small guest room, and into a large, well lit kitchen.

The smell of chicken soup met Lily's nostrils and she welcomed the comfortable feeling it invoked. But nothing else about the room or the people sitting around the large oak table felt familiar. A woman picked up a small child and put her on her lap to make room for them. Then a man with a short cap of hair like a monk's placed a plate and utensils on the table. He introduced himself as Eli, short for Eliahu. Then he nodded to his younger brother, at the end of the table, the one who had answered the door and made Lily think of Ari.

Each in turn said their name and smiled at her. The names of the two boys, *Barak* and *Raam*, Thunder and Lightning, made her smile.

Lily wanted to know why they called themselves Messianics, but she didn't ask because she didn't want them to question her in turn. She did ask if they all lived together in this house.

"No." Eli smiled with a slight upturn of his mouth. "Gideon and Miri live next door with their daughter."

"We rent a place near the main road," said Shimon.

She liked the sensible appearance of Shimon's wife, Pnina. She wore trousers and a cotton sweater, and her long dark hair was pulled back in a ponytail. Her pleasant face was framed by bangs and arched eyebrows.

Without preamble, they commenced singing. There were no instruments, but they started and stopped each song as if on cue.

During the singing, which was lively and uninhibited, Lily scrutinized each face. Miri had delicate features and a peaches-and-cream complexion. Her husband was a dark, thin-faced man who looked as if he should be in an El Greco painting. Across from them sat Shimon, a giant of a man with black hair and a full, bushy beard. He held Thunder on one knee and had his arm around Lightning.

Lily noted that no man wore a kippa, neither did the two women wear head coverings. Definitely not orthodox. But what then? They were singing in Hebrew. Eli now sat at the head of the table. Dan, the beautiful guy who had answered the door, sat at the opposite end. He shut his eyes as he sang and Lily thought he looked like a Byzantine painting of an angel, with huge almond shaped eyes and a joyfully upturned mouth. But nothing like the archangel Michael.

The music went on and on. Lily was glad that Rachel had insisted they have a late afternoon tea with sandwiches and cake. *At this rate, we won't be eating chicken before ten.*

Lily's prediction proved nearly correct. The songs stopped around nine. She pointedly looked at her watch. They took turns reading from the Bible for twenty minutes, then prayed for another ten. At least Lily thought they were praying, she didn't know enough Hebrew to be sure.

Rachel sat beside her and neither sang nor prayed, but Lily noticed Rachel's foot tapping in time to the music. Rachel smiled at Lily after the last amen. For some reason, this made Lily want to turn and dash for the back door.

Dan stood and served the chicken and dumplings. The challah was passed around the table, and each person tore off a large piece. Gideon placed a platter of saffron-colored rice on the table, then a garden salad.

Lily picked at her food, astounded to see the men serving instead of the women. Everybody seemed to talk at the same time, creating a cacophony that was not unpleasant. *These people are definitely not goyim.* Lily remembered having Sunday dinner at the home of Christian friends from school. Nobody had reached across the table to spear a hunk of butter. It had been "Please pass this" and "Would you mind handing me that?"

They all pitched in to clear the table as the teakettle boiled. A large chocolate cake appeared. Lily looked around the kitchen for an oven but found none. She noted only a two-burner gas ring on the marble counter. The dishes and pans sat on homemade shelves.

The two single men, Eli and Dan, who evidently owned the house, placed a cup, saucer, and spoon in front of each guest. Eli stood and pronounced a blessing on all present even as the clink of teaspoons against the sides of cups subsided.

Later that night, walking up the hill to Rachel's home, Lily asked the question that had tormented her all evening. "What makes them different? And don't tell me they're like you and me. Because they aren't."

"Just keep your mind open. Like I did when I first heard your story. OK?" Rachel slowed down and spoke softly. "They're Jews who believe the messiah has already come."

Lily stopped walking and turned to face Rachel. She narrowed her eyes and said, "As in Jesus Christ?"

"Uh huh."

Lily was speechless. She put her head down and started walking. The fragrance of night-blooming jasmine permeated the darkness with its unmistakable sweetness. Bats flew in and out of the trees, dive bombing for insects. Lily believed the story about bats wrapping their little hands in long hair and wished her hair was shorter.

"Everybody in Rosh Pinna knows about these Messianics?"

"It's not a secret if that's what you mean," Rachel replied.

"Are they accepted? As Jews?"

"All of us at the top of the hill don't care one way or another. The farmers are secular, and yet they act offended. I don't know why. The few orthodox Jews here in Rosh Pinna are hostile. Occasionally they throw rocks at their windows, that sort of thing."

"What is there about them that appeals to you?" Lily was curious and repelled at the same time.

"I told you, I studied the kabala. I believe there is a spiritual world. They have something about them. I can't define it." Rachel laughed. "Who are you to question them? You with your talk of archangels."

Lily wasn't about to allow any comparison between them and herself. "What makes them different from any Christian? Baptists, Catholic, whatever?"

"Who's a Jew? I'm too tired to debate such a subject. Tomorrow, perhaps." They reached the house and Rachel went directly to her studio.

Lily undressed and lay down on the couch. The pop and snap of dying embers in the fireplace could not distract her as in previous nights. She stared at the glowing coals, grateful that olive wood burned slowly through the chilly night.

She had never questioned her identity before. She was a Jew. It's something she inherited from her mother and father. She fell asleep vowing to discuss this with Rachel in the morning.

Neither Lily nor Rachel rose before noon. The Sabbath day was half over before they made a pot of coffee and went out on the verandah. Dappled sunlight played with the leaves on the ancient oak tree. Lily tossed a breadcrust to a bold squirrel who sat on his hind legs and chattered to be fed.

Lily was the first to bring up the subject of the night before. "I've never really thought about it. I'm Jewish because my parents are Jewish. Now, I come to Israel and find it's not so simple."

Rachel smiled and lifted her legs to prop them on the railing. "*Who's a Jew?* This is a hot topic in Israel. Are we a tribe?

Blood descendants of Abraham? Then how do you explain the Ethiopian Jews?"

"You're talking about the Falashim, right? I've read about the problems they're having in the absorption centers. Never saw indoor plumbing before." Lily laughed, then stopped when she saw Rachel frowning. "I can't help it."

"Their gene pool is obviously black Nubian. Yet they observed the commandments for centuries in their villages. Why airlift tens of thousands of them to Israel if they aren't true Jews?" Rachel said, as if in rebuke for Lily's laughter.

"Yeah, there are plenty of Israelis who don't observe any of the commandments," Lily replied."

"But the *datiim*, the orthodox, think none of us are Jewish enough."

Suddenly, Lily thought of Ari and his mixed gene pool and choked on her coffee.

"What's the matter, *motek*? Did you just remember your grandfather was a Cossack?" Rachel patted Lily's back.

"It's Ari," she gasped. "On his father's side he's Muslim. No one knows for sure about his mother. But he was raised by Jews. What does that make him?"

"I see your point. Is it in the blood? Genetic? Or is it culturally absorbed?"

"What about your friends down the hill? They chose another religion. Are they still Jews?"

"Hitler would have said, 'It's in the blood' and gassed them."

"Enough already. This subject is driving me crazy," Lily complained.

"Listen, Lily, when your Ari returns from wherever he is, marry him. Don't let this talk about who's a Jew confuse you. We'll be debating this issue until the Messiah comes."

"Or when Jesus returns. But seriously, do you think he's

coming back?" Lily asked.

"Jesus?"

"No. Ari. It's been months and not even a postcard from him."

"Well, didn't you say he was on a mission for the Mossad? Undercover agents don't write home."

"I didn't exactly say he was working for them. Dr. Klein was vague about it. All she said was it was a matter of national security."

"Well, there you have it. Your sweetheart is a secret agent. Just don't let him dump you at his kibbutz when he goes off on another assignment."

Lily laughed. It felt good talking about Ari even if Rachel made light of everything. Just hearing his name spoken out loud eased the ache inside her chest.

Chapter 27

Looking down the path, Lily saw Ari sitting under an oak tree. Her heart rate accelerated at the sight of his unruly, shoulder-length curls. He looked just as he had at the airport. Her thoughts raced as fast as her heart. He must have slipped into Rosh Pinna during the night. *Why is he sitting under a tree? Waiting for me?*

"Hello," he said, turning at the sound of her footsteps.

Then she saw the beard wasn't the same. Her heart fell like a stone. It was Daniel. Her face burned with disappointment. It was true, she thought, hope deferred did make the heart sick. Her knees felt weak. She half slid, then stumbled to the spongy moss beside him.

He put out his arm to steady her. His hand felt cool and dry on her bare arm.

Lily willed herself to hide her emotions. "I'm all right. A bit woozy from the heat."

Dan gestured toward the shimmering waves emanating off the white boulders in the wadi. "*Hamsin*," he said. "Hot winds from Saudi Arabia."

"I hike here nearly every morning. Never met anyone before," she said, a slight tremor in her voice.

"Perhaps we were destined to meet."

Lily looked up puzzled. "What do you mean?"

"Our paths crossing is a good thing. We really didn't get acquainted Friday night."

Lily shrugged, then stretched her legs into a more comfortable sitting position, pulling her long skirt over her ankles.

Dan picked a tiny cyclamen growing in a crevice of a nearby rock and handed it to her. "I could tell by your face that you thought I was somebody else."

"And I thought I had a poker face," Lily said, gazing into his aqua-green eyes.

"What brings you to Rosh Pinna?" Dan asked.

"Just visiting. I know Rachel from the time we were together on a commune in California." She slipped the fragile flower behind her ear. "What's your commune like?"

Dan laughed. "We call our group a *kehila*, a congregation."

"Do you share *everything*?" Lily asked.

Daniel's raised eyebrows reminded her of the way her mother looked if she said anything with a sexual connotation at the dinner table. "You mean group sex?"

"No, I can tell you're obviously religious. I guess I'm asking if you always eat together and that kind of thing."

"Only on Friday nights. You and Rachel are always welcome."

"I don't know how long I'll be staying with Rachel. I'm waiting for someone." Lily didn't know why she was telling him this. Maybe it was his eyes, as open and translucent as a gem stone. She gazed into them and blushed.

"Come back and have lunch with us." Dan stood and brushed loose leaves off his trousers.

"Why not? It's too hot to hike any farther." Lily spoke with a determined cheerfulness. He affected her in a strange way, but she couldn't pinpoint the reason for her feelings, other than his resemblance to Ari.

The Samson Option

They strolled through the fields behind the houses, reached a vegetable garden, then walked through an unused stable and into the courtyard. She saw two doors, one on the right leading into the kitchen and a lower door on the left with three stone steps leading into a basement. The smaller door opened and Eli stepped into the sunlight, blinking as if he had been in darkness for some time.

"Lily is joining us for lunch," Dan said to his brother as they entered, one by one, the kitchen.

Lily sat alone at the oak table while the brothers sliced cheese, bread, and tomatoes. She noticed a mural painted on the wall, lush vines, leaves, and clusters of purple grapes. Someone had meticulously hand-painted ornate Hebrew letters. She decided she didn't want to know what it said. There was something definitely spooky about "handwriting on the wall." What was the passage from the Book of Daniel? *Tekel, tekel, mene.* However you say it, it signifies doom.

She turned her attention to the two brothers fixing lunch. Both seemed to be in their mid-thirties. Eli was shorter and beardless, and the authoritative way he moved around the kitchen implied that he was in charge. Dan took orders from his brother with easy grace. *No sibling rivalry there, or at least they have worked it out by now.*

Eli bowed his head and gave a blessing so brief that Lily almost missed it as she popped a green olive in her mouth. She savored the pungent flavor of the home-cured olive. It was an acquired taste, nothing like the fleshy, tasteless olives she ate in America. She discreetly spit the pit into her hand and placed it on her plate. Dan passed her the bread and cheese. To make polite conversation, Lily inquired about their work.

"We sort plums at the local fruit-packing plant," Eli responded.

"That pays enough to live on?"

"It's seasonal work, but it keeps us going," Dan said.

"What do you do off season?" She wondered if they would answer in unison this time.

"We serve the Lord," Eli responded.

If they were talking about the God of Israel, and were religious Jews, they would have used the euphemistic *HaShem*, The Name. She couldn't think of an appropriate response.

They stood to clear the table, apparently not aware of the awkwardness she felt. She offered to wash up, and they vehemently protested.

"Go sit in the living room. We'll join you in a minute."

The living room contained nothing but two wooden sofa-beds with thin mattresses tightly covered in gray wool blankets. Someone had neatly tucked in the corners of the blankets, military style. Throw pillows made it possible to sit comfortably, leaning back against the wall, at least for a tall person like Lily. She noticed when Eli sat down, being short, he sat on the edge, his feet flat on the floor. Dan kicked his shoes off and pulled his feet up and sat cross-legged.

The two sofa-beds sat at right angles separated by an end table that held a vase of dried ruby-red flowers called *Jacob's Blood*. Tiny silver stars on invisible string hung from the deep-blue ceiling. Typical of the houses built in the early part of the century, the floor was hand-chiseled sandstone. Lily looked around the room with admiration. It was simple but original. One wall had ornate calligraphy painted on it, as in the kitchen. This time her curiosity got the better of her and she asked what it said.

Dan read it first in Hebrew, then translated in English. "All we like sheep have gone astray . . ."

The Samson Option

It didn't mean a thing to Lily. She felt only relief that it was not a prediction of eminent doom.

Eli said it was from the book of the prophet Isaiah but made no attempt to explain. She thought of the pencil etching from the stone stele in the convent garden. It too was ancient Hebrew prophecy. Could these brothers interpret it for her? She felt she could trust them more than the professor at the Rockefeller Museum. Aloni couldn't hide his eagerness to get his hands on the original. The greedy gleam in his eyes had repelled her.

But it was too soon to share her secret with them. She hardly knew them. They seem to have secrets of their own. What was Eli doing in the basement at midday? The way his eyes blinked when he emerged into the sunlight, he must have been down there a long time.

"Rachel tells us you speak with angels," Dan said matter-of-factly.

Lily's face froze. *Can they read my mind?* She thought of Sufis and fortune tellers, magicians that bend spoons with the power of thought. Then, anger at Rachel's indiscretion welled up inside and she found herself gasping for breath.

"Angels?" she choked out. "What do you mean by angels?"

Dan and Eli leaned forward, concern on their faces. Eli spoke first. "We didn't mean to upset you. Rachel mentioned something about the archangel Michael."

"We know something about angels," Dan added. "But if you prefer, we can talk about something else."

Lily forced a swallow. "No, go ahead," she said in a barely audible voice.

Dan looked to his brother for confirmation, then began. "Did you know that Satan can appear as an angel of light?" He waited for Lily to respond, and when she said nothing, he continued. "Throughout history, angels have appeared as messengers of God. The word we translate in English as angel simply means *messenger* in Hebrew. God sent these messengers to Abraham, Daniel, Joseph, and Miriam, to name just a few."

Eli interrupted his brother to add, "Muslim tradition says the angel Gabriel revealed the Koran to Mohammed."

Lily's composure returned as she listened to their rhythmic recitation. They reminded her of a certain high school teacher who lectured on arcane subjects. "What has any of this to do with me?" She crossed her arms on her chest.

Eli's sad, heavy-lidded eyes looked up at the silver stars swaying from their invisible strings. "It's important to know what kind of angel is appearing to you in your dreams."

Lily sniffed. "You're asking me if I talk with an angel of light as opposed to an angel of darkness?"

"Something like that."

"How do you think I know? You tell me." Suspicion blazed from Lily's hazel eyes.

"Well," Dan hesitated a moment as if he contemplated changing the subject. "What do you and Michael talk about?"

Lily felt cornered. "What's it to you?" She replied, immediately feeling childish. *Why can't I talk about this like an adult?*

"It's no big deal." Eli got up as if to signal an end to the visit.

"No, wait," Lily blurted out. "Michael told me to come to Israel. After I got here, he told me in a dream to visit the Russian convent in Ain Karem."

Eli sat down. "You don't have to tell us this."

"I know, but now I want to." She needed affirmation of her nocturnal visitations, and she sensed that these brothers might be the ones to give it to her.

Dan shook his head. "What did he tell you to find? The ark of the covenant?"

"In fact, no." Lily sat forward on the edge of the sofa-bed.

"That's a relief," Eli said.

"Why?"

"Because searchers of the ark, or the holy grail, are on a wild goose chase."

"Inspired by the angel of light, Satan?" Lily knew she sounded sarcastic, but she meant to convey her perplexity.

"Well, yes, to be blunt. But tell us, what did you find in the convent?"

Impetuously, Lily decided to reveal all. She took an envelope from her pocket then removed the pencil etching, and smoothed it out before handing it to Dan. He in turn handed it to his brother.

Eli read it silently, then repeated it out loud. "Watch for Melchi Zedek, the King of Salem, who will appear in the end of days." He exchanged a meaningful glance with his brother, then handed the paper back to Lily.

"What do you think it means?" Lily asked.

There was a long silence. Lily could hear the breeze blowing in the cypress tree outside the window. In the distance she could hear children playing ball in the street.

Eli stood, then Dan followed. "Come, we want to show you something." They led the way through the kitchen door to the back courtyard.

Lily hesitated, then held back. She planted her feet on the cobblestones. She wasn't sure she wanted to follow the brothers into that dark, windowless basement.

Chapter 28

The melon truck crossed the desert in record time, considering the poor state of both the road and the vehicle. The driver had dumped Ari in Bandar Abbas, like one of his burlap bags of produce. Bandar Abbas was a large shipping port where tanker ships arrived empty and left filled with crude oil, the black gold of the desert.

The fisherman's hut stank of rotten bait and unwashed garments. Ari sat on a coil of heavy rope, the kind used to secure large vessels to the dock. The Mossad agent had said he would return within the hour. Ari glanced at his watch. Faint beams of light filtered through the filthy window, casting just enough illumination for Ari to make out the time. Four hours had passed. He heard footsteps passing outside the hut.

The door opened. Gripping the gun in his jacket pocket, Ari crouched in a defensive position. The fetid air in the hut sucked in the fresh sea breeze. Ari inhaled deeply, ignoring the whiff of benzene from the refineries.

The metal door banged shut behind the Israeli agent. He wore the drab cotton trousers and tunic of a dock worker. His biceps bulged against the sleeves. His shoes were castoffs made for smaller, more delicate feet, with the leather crushed down on the heel to allow his foot to slide in like a slipper.

"We've got problems," the man said without preamble. He pulled a pack of cigarettes from his pocket, offered one to Ari, who started to refuse, then changed his mind. They both lit up.

The man spoke with the cigarette in his mouth, "Khomeini's people got here before we did. Not one blasted fisherman will smuggle you across tonight."

"At any price?" Ari had hoped to leave the stinking hut and be on the water by midnight. He thought of Reza and Ferideh. Were they having similar problems at the Turkish border? Would their forged documents hold up to scrutiny? Did they have enough money to bribe the border guards? Or did fear of Khomeini curb the guards' greed? Bile burned in his throat as he imagined them, brother and sister, twisting at the end of a rope, in some God-forsaken prison yard.

"They're scared. These fishermen are simple men. The more money I offered, the more the whites of their eyes showed."

"Can we steal a boat and try to navigate ourselves?" Ari felt desperate enough to try anything.

The agent, whose name Ari still didn't know and probably never would, turned his mouth down in a grimace. He looked at Ari with a puzzled expression. "Who are you anyway?"

"A Jew on assignment, same as you." Ari dropped his cigarette on the floor and crushed it with his heel. His eyes never wavered as he stared back, but he closed his fist to control the trembling of his fingers.

"The hell you are. I've received orders from Jerusalem to get you out of here at any cost. Evidently I'm expendable, but you're not."

Ari inwardly winced at the man's words. *How much more of this craziness can I take? I'm no one special. Why do they think otherwise? First the Brotherhood, now even the Mossad.* He nervously stroked the lion-shaped scar on his cheek, then took a deep breath

"We escape together. I'm not leaving Iran unless you're with me." Ari could see relief in the Mossad agent's eyes.

"There is one more option. I've never used it before. The agent spoke with dogged determination. "Years ago headquarters planted a sleeper on a Japanese ship. Poor *freier*, the sucker's been crewing on an oil tanker for years. Tonight he gets a chance to serve his country." The agent laughed at the irony.

"He can smuggle us on to an oil tanker?" Ari didn't look convinced.

"You'll see. I'll be back by midnight." He opened the door and slipped out before Ari could react.

In true Israeli fashion, the agent was late. Ari sat in pitch darkness, with not even a ray of moonlight. One by one, he expended his matches to look at his watch. One thirty, and he had only one match left. His backside ached from his cramped position. He stood and swung his arms in a circular motion, first in one direction then the other. He used his last match to light another cigarette.

At quarter to two, the door slowly opened. "Follow me," the agent whispered.

They passed through the fishermen's wharf without encountering a soul. The fishermen obviously smelled trouble in the air and had stayed home. A sharp breeze caused lines and unfurled masts to clang and rattle. They crossed a paved road and headed across the sand dunes packed hard by wind and sun, then climbed a small hill. Before reaching the top they dropped down and crawled on hands and knees to avoid showing a silhouette on the skyline.

On the summit, Ari could see the red lights of oil tankers anchored in the harbor below. He counted five ships.

"Which tanker are we boarding?" Ari whispered.

"Patience, my friend."

Ari hated the enforced passivity and despaired of being virtually in the dark. He remembered how he'd made his way over the lava beds on the Golan by using his wits. Now his life was in this other man's hands, and he didn't even know his name.

"At least tell me your first name," he whispered as they lay on their stomachs on the sand hill.

"Dudu," the agent replied.

"Glad to make your acquaintance, Daveed," Ari said using the formal name rather than the diminutive. "Next year in Jerusalem."

Daveed chuckled low in his throat at hearing the ancient promise Jews said to each other on the Passover. "Yeah, I'll meet you for a drink in Ben Yehuda Street when this is over."

A pinprick of light flashed on and off in the harbor.

"That's our signal. Our contact is waiting for us in a lifeboat. Let's go."

They approached the pier with caution. Four jeeps, parked haphazardly near the entrance, warned them that the military police were guarding the waterfront. They could see the weak glow of the soldiers' flashlights. Crawling from shadow to shadow, they made their way to the water's edge and slipped in between the pilings. Ari braced himself for the chill water but it was comfortable, nearly the same temperature as the air.

Ari followed Daveed and waded up to his chest, then silently breast-stroked into deeper water. Gentle waves rolled over his shoulders. Two hundred meters from the shore, a modern fiberglass lifeboat dipped and swayed with the current.

Strong arms reached in the water and pulled Daveed, then

Ari into the boat. Ari brought his fingers to his lips and licked the oily water.

"Benzene," he whispered.

The stranger nodded. "Strip your clothes off and throw them into the sea," he said.

Ari slipped Lily's ring out of his pocket and put it in his mouth. Then he pulled his clothes off, tossed them away and crouched, shivering from more than the cold air. Raw fear gripped his insides. The lifeboat was floating in a large oil slick. One spark from the engines would blow them to pieces. *After all I've been through, to die in an inferno?*

The stranger tossed him a pair of trousers and a sweatshirt. He must know something I don't, Ari thought as he covered his nakedness.

Daveed also put on fresh clothes and motioned for Ari to take a seat in the stern. "Next stop Oman," Daveed whispered.

The stranger took a lighter out of his pocket, then tapped a cigarette out of a pack. He lit it, took one long drag and tossed the glowing butt in the sea.

Ari's throat constricted in a shriek so loud that even the soldiers on the pier heard it and shivered. Fire spread across the oil slick. Voices shouted from the pier. Sirens pierced the air. Lights appeared on the oil tankers as watchmen sounded the alarm. Flames were already licking at the edges of the lifeboat.

The agent that Daveed called "the sleeper" turned the keys in the ignition and the powerful twin engines roared into life. They floated in a sea of flames. Ari looked with despair at Daveed.

"Next year in Jerusalem!" Daveed shouted above the roar of the engines.

Is he mad? Ari bitterly regretted putting his life in the hands of the Mossad. He wanted to grab Motti Pincus' skinny white neck and squeeze till his eyes bulged. "Trust us," Pincus had said. "We'll get you out."

Ari thought of Lily. He would never give her the ring, now safe in his pocket again. They would never have a life together. He grieved for Reza and Ferideh, the family he never knew, and fervently hoped they had made it across the border. He would now never avenge his parents' death. Tears blurred his vision. Great drops of water rolled down to his chin and dripped onto his sweatshirt. Stunned, he put his hands out and felt the shower of cold, salty water. This was more than his tears.

He saw Daveed laughing like a maniac. Great spouts of water shot into the air and fell on the lifeboat. A constant stream of sea water bathed them as the boat escaped out of the harbor unscathed, heading for the coast of Oman.

Halfway across the gulf, Daveed explained their miraculous escape. "Our colleague here stole this newfangled lifeboat. It's equipped to take the crew off a burning oil tanker. It pumps sea water over the boat. We also have pure oxygen at our disposal."

"He deliberately poured the fuel on the water?" Ari leaned his head in the direction of the man piloting the boat.

"Just like I told him to." Daveed grinned. "He wants to go home as much as we do."

Ari doubted that. No one could be more eager to be going home than himself.

"*Toda l' El!*" Ari shouted and whooped as he thanked God for his life.

"Thank our friend, here. I don't know how much God had to do with it." Daveed laughed in relief as he pounded Ari on the back.

Chapter 29

The midday haze glowed like a dimming lantern. Jerusalemites, obliged to venture outside their homes, held dampened handkerchiefs to their noses to filter the gritty air. The hamsin, a particularly nasty desert dust storm, would continue for days.

Ari sat in the back seat of the government-issue black Volvo. The struggling air-conditioner strained the engine to the point of overheating. The driver punched the off button. His eyes met Ari's in the rear-view mirror, not in apology, but more in a question.

"It's okay," Ari reassured the driver. He preferred to open the car window and smell the pine-scented air of the Jerusalem forest. Even the heavy wind blowing in from the Sinai was like the dew from heaven to a man just returned from enemy territory.

He wondered why Motti Pincus didn't personally meet him. Then he remembered the legion of foreign and domestic undercover agents milling around Ben Gurion International Airport.

On his flight from Oman to Heathrow he thought he had detected a fellow Israeli, dressed as an American businessman. The nervous way the man smoked one cigarette after another, even though the steward asked him not to smoke, gave him away. Pincus had said "We'll cover you," and he proved true to his word.

Ari now leaned back on the plush upholstery of the Volvo. The car reached the western entrance to Jerusalem and continued east on Jaffa Road. Three blocks from the Old City, the driver pulled into the narrow lane beside the Jerusalem police headquarters known as the Russian Compound. Ari knew he was returning to the nondescript two-story building, behind Barclays Bank, which served as the Mossad's headquarters in the capital of Israel.

He expected the car to stop at the front entrance but showed no surprise when they eased into an alley, built for donkey carts by the looks of it. Ari wondered how much paint would be scraped off the sides of the vehicle, but the driver evidently knew this route well. He continued to the end of the alley without incident. Then the driver punched a button on his sun visor. A metal gate opened. He parked the car in a makeshift carport and Ari followed him inside.

A woman took over and led Ari up the back steps to the second floor. He once again found himself in the room where Motti Pincus had recruited him. He recognized the unadorned wooden table and the samovar bubbling on the sideboard. He could detect the smell of a damp mop hurriedly swished over a dusty tile floor.

Ari was grateful to be back in Israel. At the same time, he didn't look forward to telling Pincus about Iran's plans to bring about nuclear holocaust. He knew he would sound like a modern day Jeremiah, predicting disaster of a magnitude so great they wouldn't believe him. The Mossad had sent him to Tehran to find the facts about their biological warfare capabilities. He had also found evidence of that.

Ari stood at the window looking at swirling gusts of fine sand. He turned as the door opened and Motti Pincus entered, followed by two men. He saw Pincus' eyes light up with recognition and relief. It quickly changed to a professional mask.

"Welcome back, Ari. I trust you had a good time?" Pincus pounded him on the back with the forced familiarity of a school reunion. "My colleagues are eager to hear about your holiday adventure." He did not introduce the two men who quietly took their seats at the table.

Pincus folded his tall, lanky body into a chair and motioned Ari to sit. He faced the two others who, in contrast to Pincus' height and pale complexion, were short and swarthy. Both men sat with their hands on the table.

"Don't know where to start," Ari mumbled.

"Start at the beginning where this Reza fellow comes to your hotel room and has tea with you. Leave nothing out," Pincus said.

Ari stiffened. How did Pincus know he'd had tea with Reza in his hotel room that first night in Tehran? Could the waiter have been Mossad? Pincus apparently knew every detail of where he had gone in Iran and everyone he had talked to. Did Pincus know about his blood relationship to Reza? Had the Mossad known all along about his birth father? Is that why they were so willing to risk sending an amateur? He stroked the lion-shaped scar on his cheek.

Pincus stared at him. The other two men sat like statues. They might not have been in the room for all the stir they caused. Even their breathing was undetectable. The only sound was the moan and sigh of the wind trying to penetrate the metal shutters on the window.

Stalling for time while he decided how to give his account, Ari got up and poured himself a cup of tea from the teapot warming on the samovar. It looked dark and bitter, so he added four lumps of sugar. "Any milk?"

"Milk?" Pincus frowned. When the older man nodded at him, he hurried out the door to get milk.

Ari stood at the sideboard, secretly pleased that Pincus had to fulfill his whim. He studied the faces of the two sitting at the table. One had snowy white hair brushed straight back in the old Russian style. His deeply lined forehead made him look as if he'd spent his days poring over dusty ledgers in an accounting house. Ari sensed he wasn't a bookkeeper, but he looked like one.

The other man looked much younger. Maybe in his mid-thirties, with a short, American-style crew cut. The haircut didn't fit his long, narrow face. He looked Middle Eastern, with prominent eyebrows and almond shaped eyes, the kind seen in Persian miniatures. Ari guessed that the older one was the Head of Station and the younger man his resident expert on Iran.

It seemed to be taking Pincus a long time to find Ari's milk. He probably had to send a subordinate out to the local *mokelet* to buy some. After what seemed like half an hour but was only minutes, Pincus re-entered the room and poured milk into Ari's tea, which by now had grown cold.

Ari left the tea on the sideboard, and took his seat again. The older man smiled agreeably as if he knew Ari was stalling and didn't care.

"Reza introduced me to the Ayatollah Zaheydeh, as planned," Ari began without preamble. "This was in Qom. Then Zaheydeh sent me to a military base in the Caspian region where I met Colonel Melekzadeh."

Ari noticed that no one was taking notes, so he assumed they were taping the conversation. He recited from memory the coordinates of the Shah's hunting palace, the number and condition of roads and troops. He described in detail the underground bunker and the Russian technicians.

"This confirms it. They *are* preparing for biological warfare," said the agent with the Persian features. His tone suggested vindication.

The white-haired man unclasped his hands and raised his palms up as if in supplication. He spoke in a low, controlled voice. "Anything else?"

Ari decided he would not volunteer any information about Reza and Ferideh. If the Mossad already knew they were his half-brother and half-sister it didn't matter. If they didn't know, he wasn't going to tell them. In any event, what he had to say about Iran's nuclear weapons outweighed the details of his personal situation.

He swallowed hard, regretting that he had left the tea on the sideboard. His mouth was as dry as the fine sand blowing in from the Sinai. "They have nuclear capabilities, thanks to Russia, and they seem willing to use them. Right now it's a matter of obtaining long-range missiles capable of hitting Tel Aviv."

"Yes," the head agent replied softly. "We know about their nuclear weapons program. Do they know about ours?"

A chill passed over Ari, causing him to tremble. "I mentioned Israel's nuclear plant in Dimona. Little Satan could retaliate. Might even send a preemptive strike against Tehran, I told them. Colonel Melekzadeh only laughed when he heard this."

Ari looked to see how the three men at the table would respond. All three presented a blank stare, but Ari thought he detected a flicker of anxiety from Pincus.

"What do you think his scorn means?" Asked the senior man.

Ari's voice broke with constrained emotion. "Ever heard of *qorban*?"

Only the specialist in Iranian affairs nodded. Ari figured that he was an Iranian Jew, now an Israeli citizen.

The winds from the Sinai rattled the shutters. The air in the room had become warm and stifling.

"Shi'ites are raised on the story of Imam Hussein's martyrdom. They reenact his bloody death every year during Moharram. They tell the story over and over in their mosques and in their homes. Personal sacrifice is in their mothers' milk, according to Colonel Melekzadeh."

"What exactly are you saying?" Pincus' face looked pinched and paler than usual.

"It's simple," Ari replied. "Iran has over sixty-five million people. Israel's population is only six million. If they drop atomic bombs on us, we retaliate. When the dust clears, who will be left standing?"

It was a rhetorical question and Ari expected no answer. Still, in the painful silence that sucked the life out of the air, he felt compelled to speak.

"That's where *qorban*, sacrifice, comes in. They are willing to sacrifice millions of their people if it means they will wipe out the Jews."

The senior agent reached in his pocket for his pipe. "The Samson Option in reverse." He punched the tobacco down with his thumb, struck a match and inhaled the acrid smoke. "The Colonel said that, did he? You're absolutely sure there was no mistake in the translation?" With his thumb and forefinger he crushed the match stick.

"His exact words," Ari replied. He looked from face to face with growing admiration for the self-control exhibited by these men. If he could have looked in a mirror he knew his own face would look strained with anxiety. He knew what the Samson Option meant.

"We have a complete dossier on Colonel Melekzadeh. He served the Shah for fifteen years, then switched allegiance to Khomeini in a matter of minutes. A shrewd and pragmatic man. I think we can take him at his word."

The Head of Station stood, his shoulders rounded with more than age and fatigue. "We didn't tell you everything we know, Ari. But now, since you have heard about it directly, I can reveal that we knew Germany began building a reactor in Bushehr in 1974, under the pro-Western Pahlavi regime. Germany dropped out in 1979 when Khomeini came to power. We are aware that the Russians took over the project."

"Can't you stop the Russians"? Ari asked in amazement.

"Not even the Americans could stop the Russian minister of atomic energy from signing an agreement worth more than one billion dollars. Russia needs the money."

Pincus gave Ari a look of pity mixed with cold reality. He spoke softly, with an air of resignation. "The Western powers do nothing even when the Iranian leaders publicly renounce the establishment of Israel as the most hideous occurrence in Middle East history. They say things like, we will vomit her out from our midst, and the Zionist regime is a cancerous tumor."

Pincus sensed that Ari had heard more than he wanted to know. He reached out and shook Ari's hand. "You are free to go home. We know where to reach you."

Ari felt no relief, only a sense of crushing fatigue. Pincus walked him to the back door. Ari was amazed at how quickly the debriefing had gone. Then he looked at his watch. Four hours had passed. His system was still working on an adrenaline overload. He knew it would be days or weeks before he could sort out his emotions. For now he chose to put it all away, far away.

The same driver who had picked Ari up at the airport drove him down Jaffa Road to the Central Bus Station and pulled over to the curb. Ari got out and watched the black Volvo disappear in the traffic. Had he expected them to send him back to the kibbutz in a luxury car? No, he knew the unspoken rules. Even the Entebbe heroes had hitchhiked from Ben Gurion airport to their homes after their return from that infamous rescue raid in Africa.

He had only one thought now. Find Lily. He didn't go into the bus terminal and catch a bus north as the Mossad would expect. Instead, he walked over to the number twenty-six bus stop and waited for the next bus to Ain Karem.

Lily should still be in the rented house across from the Russian convent. If she wasn't there, Dr. Klein would know where she went. He lit a cigarette. While he waited for his bus, he wondered ruefully if Pincus knew about Lily.

Chapter 30

Daniel stood in the basement doorway, his head cocked and eyebrows raised as if to ask *are you coming in or not?* Lily saw no coercion in his expression. She knew the choice was hers. She also knew this decision was irrevocable. It would change her life if she followed the brothers and entered the subterranean room.

She looked up to the sky, hoping for an omen. The faded blue, cloudless heavens disappointed her. In the distance, she heard the drone of Israeli jets avoiding Syrian airspace by roaring up the narrow finger of the Upper Galilee. What would the archangel Michael expect her to do?

More realistically, what would Ari want her to do? Thinking of him steadied her nerves. If only he would come back, she thought. He would help her sort out the meaning of the black stone.

She stood mute with indecision as the hot afternoon sun beat on her uncovered head like a fist. Rivulets of sweat ran down the small of her back, soaking the waist band of her skirt. The dark shadows behind Daniel began to look cool and inviting rather than menacing.

Daniel smiled and reached out to steady her as she stepped down into the cavernous room underneath the house. The air was cool and dry, suffused with the smell of ancient stone and melted beeswax.

She stood just inside the doorway until her eyes adjusted to the dim light coming from one thick, short candle burning on a stone ledge. She made out the figure of Eli, sitting on a small, four-legged stool. Dan took her hand, indicating that she should sit next to his brother. Then he sat facing them.

Lily picked up a faint horsy smell coming from the coarse camel-hair carpet underneath her feet. *Nothing sinister here*, she thought. *It smells like a clean stable. How does that song go, "Away in a Manger"?* Her mother had never let her participate in school pageants, but she'd memorized the songs along with her classmates.

What am I afraid of? It isn't physical danger that made me hesitate in the courtyard. They intend to convince me that Jesus Christ is the Jewish messiah. It's not enough to be a mashugana. *I should also be a* boged, *a traitor?*

Eli spoke first. Lily noted the younger brother always yielded to the elder.

"Lily, my brother and I believe that you are one of the chosen who will rebuild the fallen tabernacle of David. We want you to consider joining us."

Lily sighed in relief. *Not a word about J.C.* She knew there must be more, so she remained silent.

"God is gathering an army to stand in the last days," Daniel said.

Her interest heightened at the mention of the end times. Their audacity in boldly pronouncing the word God, with no euphemistic *The Name*, or even *The Lord*, secretly pleased her. She never did like that humble-pie, beating-around-the-bush style that was her father's.

"What do you mean by the *fallen tabernacle of David*?" Lily asked, squirming on the hard wicker stool.

"We call this place," Eli glanced around indicating the space they were in, "Adullam's Cave."

Daniel spoke next in the way close siblings and long-married couples complete each other's thought. "A band of friends, relatives, and plain old malcontents gathered around David in the years before he came into his kingdom. They hid in the wilderness of Ain Gedi, in a cave called Adullam."

"And the fallen tabernacle?" Lily asked once again.

"The fallen tabernacle, or tent, is where David set up the ark, the place where he worshipped God. *The House of David* is a metaphor for Israel. We, as a nation, have fallen into a state of spiritual decay." Daniel's eyes glowed with an intensity that lit his entire face, making him more attractive than ever to Lily.

She tried to concentrate on what he was saying, but to do that she would have to avoid his stunning green eyes. She turned to face Eli, whose plain countenance helped still her agitated nerves. *What does this have to do with me?*

As if reading her thoughts, Eli said, "The archangel Michael is Israel's protector. Michael has apparently led you to a monument from the tomb of King David."

Lily swallowed hard, wishing she had a glass of cool water. "Is it possible that the ark of the covenant is buried there in Ain Karem? Rachel seems to think so."

"My brother and I don't believe anybody will find the ark. Hollywood likes the theme, Indiana Jones and all that. But Scripture indicates that the ark is in heaven," Eli said matter-of-factly.

Lily's eyes widened in astonishment. "What scripture are you reading?"

Daniel looked at his brother, as if for confirmation, then replied, "When the Apostle John was exiled to the island of

Patmos, he had a vision of heaven and saw the ark."

Lily blinked rapidly. "John? Patmos?"

"You've probably never read the book of Revelation."

"Sure haven't," Lily snapped. They should have known that.

"Lily, this chamber, which we refer to as our *cave of Adullam*, it's our shul, you might say. It's where we pray and meditate. We worship the God of Israel, the God of our fathers, Abraham, Isaac, and Jacob."

"There is more, isn't there?" she asked quietly.

"Yes. Rachel told you that we believe that Jesus is the messiah. We also believe that the end times are near, that he is coming back soon. You have come here with this message about Melchizedek. It confirms what we already know."

"Who is this Melchizedek guy?" Lily firmly turned the conversation away from the *Jesus as messiah theme*.

"Well," Eli hesitated. "We didn't intend to go into all this, but . . ."

Daniel finished his sentence. "He is a type and shadow of Jesus."

"It keeps coming back to him." Lily felt annoyed but tried to hide it.

"You could say that. Listen, we truly would like you to join us. We know it sounds confusing, just think it over."

Lily rose, politely announcing her intention to leave. The brothers followed her out into the courtyard and said goodbye. She thanked them for lunch and rushed off into the fields behind their house.

Following the curve of the hillside, she headed back to the wadi. The afternoon sun had burned the sky to an ash white. Locusts chirped in the dry grass.

She followed the wadi upstream until she came to a natural pool. The water flowed down an embankment in a miniature waterfall, then collected in a deep granite basin. As she stopped to catch her breath, she observed how the placement of large boulders provided a sense of privacy.

She stood motionless staring into the still water. After a moment of hesitation, she slipped off her sandals, unbuttoned her skirt, letting it drop on the ground, and pulled her tee-shirt over her head. She hesitated then stepped into the water, submerging herself to her chin. With the sudden change of body temperature she felt a pleasant sensation of euphoria. Floating on her back, with only her face above water, Lily closed her eyes and let her mind wander.

With the clarity that happens only in books, or so she thought, she felt herself leaving her body. She found herself hovering twenty feet in the air, gazing down at her body floating in the leaf-strewn pool. Her closed eyelashes fluttered on her tan cheeks. The water covered all but her face and toes. It thrilled her to find that she could be in two places at once—her physical body in the water and her spirit hovering above.

No sooner did that concept cross her mind than she was back in her body, floating in the water. For the first time in her life she believed, really believed, that there was an afterlife. Even though she had always prayed on Yom Kippur and felt herself included in the "book of life," this prayer always bothered her because it implied that she might not be included. She had never given much, if any, thought to life after death. Like many of her contemporaries, she believed in doing good deeds, here and now, with no talk of heaven.

But, I am more than this physical body. This thought pleased her enormously. Drifting in the gentle ebb and flow of the pool, she reviewed the day's events. She considered Eli and

Daniel's invitation to join their group. What will Rachel say? *Does she believe Jesus is the messiah?*

Lily pulled herself out of the water and lay on a flat, sun-heated boulder to dry. The warm air blew over her skin in a silken caress. Then the heat became too much and she put on her clothes and returned to Rachel's house.

"Are you crazy?" Rachel sounded annoyed rather than angry. "I introduced you to those people because I thought you needed some diversion. Not so you'd join them!" She picked up her piecework and stabbed the needle in and out of the material.

"They understand me." Lily's statement sounded lame even to herself.

"What about Ari? I thought you wanted to get married?"

"Yes, Ari. What about him? He's gone. Kaput. Finito. Disappeared without a trace. My dream lover. No more make believe. He's not my fiancé. I made that up." Hot, fat tears spilled down her face in contradiction to her words.

"Don't delude yourself that something might happen between you and Daniel. He and his brother practice celibacy. Believe me, I know." Rachel bit the end off the knotted thread.

"Celibacy?" The word hung in the air like a fragile soap bubble about to pop.

"Both have taken a vow never to marry." Rachel paused to let her words sink in. "No sex, no nothing. And before I begin to sound like your mother, I'm going to bed." Rachel put her sewing in a large, flat basket on the floor.

"I'm not attracted to Dan." Even as she said it, she knew it wasn't true.

"Lily, I don't want you to get hurt."

Alone in the sitting room that was now her bedroom, Lily undressed and put on an oversized tee-shirt. The moonlight was strong, so she closed the heavy drapes at the window. Then she lay on the sofa and tucked the velvet throw pillow under her head. After a minute, she sat up and reversed her position to the other end of the sofa. Sleep would not come.

She rose and drew the curtains back. A fragile breeze flowed across her damp neck. Rachel's last words weighed heavily on her mind.

Chapter 31

Lily's clothes lay strewn over Rachel's old couch. Piece by piece she stuffed her belongings into a denim shoulder bag: three tee-shirts, three skirts, two pair of trousers, two blouses, a dozen plain cotton panties, perfume, a comb, and toothbrush. She left a note on the kitchen table thanking Rachel for her hospitality.

The fresh, clean air of dawn left gentle traces of dew on the oleander bush beside the front door. Lily took the departure of the heat wave as confirmation to move on. She would still see Rachel, she told herself. The brothers' house was only down the lane. It took five minutes to walk from Rachel's house to theirs.

Would Eliahu and Daniel be awake? Were they expecting her? Had her sudden departure yesterday caused them to reconsider their invitation?

She opened the front gate, walked to the door, then changed her mind and followed the path around to the back. She heard the clatter of cups and silverware landing on a wooden table. A teakettle whistled in the background.

Just as she raised her hand to rap on the door, Eli stepped out from the basement.

"Good morning. Just in time for breakfast," Eli smiled. "Come inside."

Lily noted they set the table as if they were expecting her. Three cups, three plates, three butter knives, and three teaspoons. She didn't know whether she should feel flattered or suspicious, so decided to be both as she sat down at the table.

She took a slice of fresh brown bread and spread it with white cheese. After a bite, she asked, "Who gets up before dawn to bake bread?"

"It's baked nightly by military bakers for soldiers and for civilians as well," Dan replied. "I usually go get it."

"Rachel makes her own bread. I've never baked so much as a biscuit." She sipped her bitter, black coffee.

After breakfast, Dan led Lily through the sitting room with the hanging stars, then into a smaller room that opened off the main room. It held a single bed, a chair, and a reading lamp.

"Like it?" Dan asked as if he were a hotel clerk.

Lily looked around for a place to store her belongings but saw no closet or chest of drawers. She smiled at Dan. "It's fine."

He left her. When the door closed behind him, Lily saw three nails, with large heads, protruding from the back of the door. "Here's where I hang my wardrobe," she said wryly.

Unpacking her few belongings became more than a simple physical act. It symbolized her desire to start over. She tried, but failed, to put thoughts of Ari behind her as she hung up her clothes. She still loved him, always would, but it was time to grow up. Unrequited love was for teenagers, she mused. He might never come back to Israel. All manner of things could have happened to him during the past months. He might have fallen in love with someone he met while on assignment.

She shook the wrinkles out of her favorite skirt before hanging it on a nail. The fabric was a pleasing confusion of multicolored hand-stitched squares. Rachel had helped her piece it together. Lily felt a twinge of guilt as she thought of Rachel reading her note. She should have told her to her face. No, Rachel might have talked her out of moving here.

With her few clothes hanging on the nails and the rest of her belongings stuffed under a chair, Lily tried out the bed. As she stretched out on the top cover she imagined her mother saying, "You've made your bed, now lie in it."

It will be just fine, thank you, Ma.

Her mother would approve of her friendship with Eliahu and Daniel, good Jewish boys whose family had immigrated from Iraq. Jews returning from the Babylonian exile would appeal to her father's sense of justice. Either of them were the kind of men her parents hoped she would one day marry, without the Jesus nonsense, of course.

Her mother never would have approved of Ari. Just as well that Lily had given up all hope of marrying him. Her father would have liked him, though. "A diamond in the rough. He'll shape up after you smooth off the raw edges of the kibbutz," she imagined her father saying. Both her parents tended to speak in clichés, which made it easy for her to imagine their reactions.

"You want us to have a son-in-law who is half Arab and half Jewish? Muslim grandchildren? *Hos va hallilyah!* God forbid," her mother would say putting her hand to her ample bosom.

Lying on her bed, Lily laughed until tears came, accompanied by heaving sobs, the tears running down her face and dripping in her ears. Ordinarily, this would have made her laugh, but not now. Remembering Ari made her heart ache with a physical pain like a throbbing bruise.

A gentle tapping on the bedroom door caused her to sit up. She wiped the tears on her sleeve, took a deep breath. "Yes?"

"Would you like to join us in the living room?" Eli said through the closed door. His voice sounded anxious.

"I need to freshen up first," Lily responded.

In the large washroom, she splashed cold water on her red face. As she examined herself in the mirror above the sink, she resolutely told herself to shape up.

These guys don't want a weepy sad-sack joining their Adullam band of end-time heroes.

Lily didn't realize it, but she had never looked so beautiful. The long walks in the wadi had tanned her normally pale complexion to a soft, golden glow. Her cheeks were like ripe peaches. The recent tears caused her eyes to sparkle. The mauve shadows under her eyes only gave her features a more refined look. Her damp hair curled in wispy tendrils around her forehead.

She took a seat on the sofa across from the brothers. They gave no indication that they had heard her sobbing. She smiled at them and asked what was on the day's agenda.

"We've planned a *tiyul*, a small trip, to Banias at the base of Mount Hermon. You're welcome to join us," Daniel said.

It only took seconds for Lily to decide to go. She needed diversion, and a picnic beside the flowing springs at Banias would do just that.

The public bus took them north as far as Kibbutz Dan. Then they hiked the few miles to the source of the Jordan River, where natural springs fed by the melting snow from the Hermon flowed from an underground cave.

Daniel pointed out a cave where tradition said ancient tribes worshipped the druid Pan. "As pronounced in Arabic dialect, *Ban*, hence the name *Banias*," he added.

They ate lunch at a picnic table under the oak trees, where children from Druze families waded in the nearby water. Army tanks, on maneuvers between the Golan and Lebanon, idled in the public parking area while the young drivers, most of them in their early twenties, took a cigarette break.

Eli bowed his head and gave thanks for their lunch of bread and canned sardines. Lily felt peaceful in their company. A breeze off the snow-capped peaks cooled the afternoon air. When the tank column departed, dust motes swirled upward.

"Are you in the reserves?" Lily asked the brothers as they watched the tanks move out.

"My brother and I serve as medics. We both refused to carry weapons during our initial basic training," Eli replied.

Lily thought of Ari and spoke impulsively. "Ever hear about the soldier who turned in his weapon after his sergeant ordered him to bury some Palestinian boys alive?"

"I remember the incident. He was a pacifist, right?"

"Well, sort of," Lily responded. She was reluctant to tell them that she knew this soldier.

"We're not pacifists, you understand," Eli continued. "God told us not to kill our brothers, the Palestinians. We do our yearly reserve duty like everyone else."

Lily wanted to tell them about Ari. She felt they would understand his dilemma, brought up Israeli, then the trauma of finding out he was half Arab. However, she said nothing. That part of her life was over. Too bad, because they would have a lot in common with Ari.

To change the subject she asked why they had picked this particular spot for a picnic. She said nothing about the meager lunch they had just eaten, even though she would not have called a can of sardines and one loaf of bread a picnic.

"This place is also known as Caesarea Philippi. Jesus and his disciples came here," said Daniel.

His brother added, "This is where Jesus asked his disciples what people were saying about Him."

Whom do people think I am? John the Baptist, or Elias, Jeremiah, or one of the prophets? Peter answered, Thou art the messiah, the Son of the Living God.

Daniel became so excited that he stood up and spread his arms wide, then turned in a half circle. "Right here, Peter, a plain man, an uneducated Jew, received the keys to the Kingdom of heaven. Think of it."

Lily didn't know what to think.

"Now, in this age, we will receive the keys to the House of David. You're a part of this, Lily."

"Just because I found the black stone with the inscription?" She wanted to believe them. They sounded so sincere.

"And your encounters with the archangel Michael."

Playing the devil's advocate, she felt compelled to tell them that her psychiatrist, Dr. Klein, did not believe that she saw and heard the angel. "Maybe it's a manifestation of conflict between my paternal and maternal self image. Or something like that," she said, misquoting Dr. Klein.

Daniel sat down again on the wooden bench. He laughed in a delightful, unself-conscious manner and put his hand on Lily's hand. "Don't pay any attention to the words of a nonbeliever. We certainly don't. Right brother?"

Eli's mood was more somber when he spoke. "We follow the Holy Spirit's lead." Then a twinkle lit up his eyes and he announced that he felt the spirit saying it was time to move on.

It was now late afternoon. They hiked back to Kibbutz Dan and found the last bus had departed.

They waited at the bus stop with arms out, thumbs extended downward in the Israeli hitchhiker's signal, until a pickup truck stopped. The Druze driver and his passenger said they only had room for Lily. She refused. A chill ran down her spine as they drove away laughing.

"If we have to split up, one of us will go with Lily," said Eli. They all agreed.

The shadows lengthened as the day wore on. Fewer and fewer vehicles passed them, and no one stopped. Tired and thirsty, Lily regretted coming on the excursion. Then a blue Ford van passed them, slowed, and backed up.

A woman in a white head scarf leaned out the window and asked in American English, "Need a ride?"

Lily ran and opened the passenger side door. "Thanks."

Eli and Daniel climbed in the back seat next to an infant strapped in a carrier.

"What's an American woman with a baby doing on this road?" Lily blurted out.

"My husband is stationed on the Golan. This is the only chance I've had to visit with him in weeks. Where can I drop you?"

"Rosh Pinna," Lily responded.

"My name is Batya. That's my daughter Orit in the back seat."

Eli and Daniel smiled and said how pleasant it was to meet her. When she dropped them off at Rosh Pinna, they invited her and her husband to visit them sometime.

That night Lily dropped exhausted into her new bed. The sheets were clean but the quilt smelled musty. Nevertheless, she fell promptly into a deep sleep.

She dreamed that the mythic figure of Pan arose from the waterfalls of Banias. Naked babies floated on miniature rafts. Ari, not the American woman, drove the blue van. The archangel Michael sat in the passenger seat.

Chapter 32

Ari ran up the steep cobblestone lane, stopping to catch his breath when he reached the small plateau in front of the Russian convent. Opposite the convent gate, he turned onto a footpath that led to the two-story house where Lily rented a ground floor apartment. Tall, graceful trees surrounded the house, giving it the appearance of a rustic country estate. Pine needles crunched under his feet, emitting their sweet fragrance.

As he approached Lily's home, he slowed to a walk. So much had happened to him since his discharge from Bet Shalom that he felt like a different person. He wasn't the same man that Lily once admired, the ex-soldier trying to find himself. How would she feel about his pseudo status as the Shi'ite messiah? Or his role as an agent of the Mossad?

She respected the dramatic gesture he'd made, turning in his weapon to his officer. He knew she leaned to the dovish side of the political spectrum, even though she claimed to be apolitical.

Yet in the past days and months, he had made a radical turnaround. He no longer thought of himself as a pacifist, now that he knew of Iran's agenda to annihilate Israel. Would Lily believe this threat was real? Would she understand that he'd had to disappear for a time because of the Brotherhood?

Anticipation at seeing her again made his heart beat faster. As he approached her front door he noted the signs of absence. The garden chairs were stacked and covered with a tarp. Piles of leaves littered the patio. It was still daylight, yet the windows were shuttered on each side of the front door.

Rapping lightly on the metal door he called her name. Getting no response he pounded harder.

"Allo!" A woman's voice floated down from the upper story of the house. "*Me zeh?* Who's there?"

Ari looked up and located the source of the voice at an open window. A woman with a head of white curly hair and incongruously young, smooth skin leaned on the window ledge.

"I'm looking for Lily," he called

"Gone!" the woman shouted back, though Ari stood close enough to hear without her shouting.

"Where?" Ari yelled back in response.

"Ask the doctora," she responded.

"*Up there?*" Ari used the euphemism for the psychiatric clinic up the lane. No local resident called it Bet Shalom. They referred to it as *up there*, with a hint of envy in their voices because of the luxurious nature of the private clinic.

"Where else?" She laughed and shut the window.

Ari turned and ran back to the lane. As he passed the Russian convent the gate suddenly opened and a black Mercedes lurched out. He jumped aside and pounded his fist on the fender. A man in a tall monk's cap glared back at him through the rearview window as though Ari was at fault. Another passenger in the back seat also turned to stare at him. The intense look in the man's eyes gave Ari a chill of recognition. No one had stared at him like that since his enforced stay at the tekiyah in Damascus. It was the look of a fanatic.

No, it can't be, he told himself. Get focused. Intuition overrode rational thinking, putting him on full alert. He sprinted the remaining hundred meters up the steep road, his chest heaving with the exertion.

Like all ex-patients, he knew how to manipulate the lock on the gate of Bet Shalom without a key. Once in the grounds he nimbly leapt over the low stone wall that separated the garden from the path and circled to the back of the clinic. He studied the configuration of the fir trees, then climbed up to the second floor balcony.

He found the French doors leading into the library unlocked and stepped inside. He paused to allow his eyes to adjust to the dim light coming from a reading lamp. He saw the bulky figure of Dr. Klein sitting with her back to him. Her gray hair curled above the collar of her white smock as she read a book.

He knew if he startled her, she'd think the assassins had come back to finish the job. Seconds passed as he pondered the dilemma.

"Come, Ari, I know it's you," Dr. Klein said without turning.

Ari froze.

Then she turned and smiled. "You think I couldn't hear you climbing the tree? Squirrels don't breathe that loud."

"How did you know it was me?" His eyes narrowed in suspicion.

"Pincus telephoned. Said I should expect you within the hour."

"He knew I didn't go home?"

"Come, sit in the easy chair." The corners of her mouth turned down. "Don't you know the Mossad have watchers everywhere? They saw you take the bus to Ain Karem. It was an easy guess that you were coming here."

He glumly acknowledged that she was right and slumped into a chair.

"They didn't anticipate that you'd go first to Lily's place, did they?"

"But you did?" Ari asked, once again astonished by the doctor's knowledge.

"Of course. Lily told me about her feelings for you."

"She did? Where is she? Her landlady said you'd know." His mouth felt dry.

"She felt she had to get out of Ain Karem. The atmosphere here was oppressing her."

"In what way?" Ari's heart began to pound.

"It had something to do with our neighbors, the Russians. She wouldn't confide in me."

Ari flinched at the mention of the Russians. They'd nearly run him over just a few minutes ago. Yet, that was purely coincidental. They had no way of knowing he was back in Ain Karem, that he'd be on the lane at that moment. Still, the look of malevolence in the man's eyes had made his stomach turn.

"Do you know where she went?" Ari's voice took on a desperate note.

"Rosh Pinna. Said she knew an old friend who lived there. Someone from her hippie days."

"What's his name?"

"*Her* name is Rachel, as I recall."

Ari carefully weighed his options. If the Mossad knew he was back in Ain Karem, then the Brotherhood probably knew also. According to Dr. Klein, Pincus was in the dark about his relationship to Lily. So, it was likely that the Muslims had no information about his connection with her.

"I'll leave for my kibbutz tomorrow. That's the obvious next step, isn't it?" Ari looked at the doctor.

"Yes, it would seem so. Rosh Pinna is less than five kilometers away from your kibbutz." She left the sentence hanging.

"Well, that's settled. Guess I'll go home. My watchers would expect me to settle in at my kibbutz. What have you got to eat? I'm starving." Food was far from his thoughts, but a trip to the kitchen would help change the subject.

"What? Our secret service didn't feed you? What's this country coming to?" She stood.

"How many patients are here?" Ari asked before rising from his chair.

"Three, and they stay in their rooms until dinner. Always."

"The new cook?" Ari felt guilty as he asked about the replacement of the murdered cook.

Dr. Klein spoke softly. "I've hired a lady from the village to cook lunch and dinner. She's on her afternoon break, won't be back before six." They took the back stairs to the first floor.

In the kitchen she put on the teakettle for coffee, then opened the refrigerator and pulled out a cheesecake. She cut two large pieces and put one before Ari.

"It's good to be back," Ari said with his mouth full.

"Can you tell me where you've been?" With her fork she sliced off one bite of cake.

He knew Pincus would want him to keep silent, but his bleak discovery in Iran was too much to carry alone. Still he procrastinated by drinking his coffee. Then he cleared the table of the dirty dishes. Finally he settled down and began to speak in a low voice.

"While on assignment for Pincus . . . I can't tell you where, you understand?"

She nodded, "Of course."

"I stumbled across some information that's hard to accept." He shivered as if he saw a ghost.

Dr. Klein looked neither sad nor pained, merely resigned.

"I've survived numerous wars and the ritual murder of my colleague. There isn't anything you can tell me that I can't deal with."

Ari sighed deeply. *Qorban*. Ritual sacrifice. The Iranians could wipe Israel off the map in a matter of hours.

"Are you aware that there are governments that have the power to destroy us?" Ari continued without letting her answer. "Even though they know we're capable of nuclear retaliation?"

Dr. Klein slipped a pack of cigarettes out of her jacket pocket, lit one and took a long drag before replying. "The Samson Option."

"What?"

"You recall the early Israelite hero. Blinded and in chains, he brought down the Gaza temple on himself and Israel's Philistine enemies?"

"Yeah, I know the story. He died, but not before he took them out."

"The State of Israel could be defeated, but it would not be overrun without wide-scale destruction of the Arab states as well. Thus we have the Samson Option. They'll go down with us." She stabbed out her cigarette in the ashtray.

"I'm not talking about an Arab state. It's Iran. They have a population of more than sixty-five million. Israel has less than six million. They're willing to gamble that they'll be the only ones standing when it's all over."

"This is why Pincus needed you so desperately?"

"I was sent to Tehran to investigate their chemical and biological warfare capabilities. I'm speaking in strict confidence, of course."

"I understand," she replied.

"They're building supplies of biological weapons. Even worse, they're close to having nuclear weapons, thanks to the

Russians. All they need now is the long-distance missile technology."

"What's that word you used, *qorban*?"

"I was told by an Iranian colonel that *qorban*, or sacrifice, is in their mothers' milk. Iran's leaders are willing to sacrifice millions of their people if it means the total destruction of Israel."

"God forbid!" Dr. Klein spoke in a grim tone. "It simply can't come to that."

"Pincus knows that our nuclear program will no longer deter them."

"The prognosis is grim, but we always survive." She paused for a long moment. "Ari, you must find Lily, get married, and raise children."

Dr. Klein stared at her strong hands with the bitten fingernails. Then she quoted a biblical passage in Hebrew, "And the remnant that is escaped of the house of Judah shall yet again take root downward, and bear fruit upward."

"Who said that?"

"The prophet *Yesheyahu*, Isaiah."

Ari raised his head and spoke softly. "Why didn't you marry and have children?"

Dr. Klein sighed. "Not all who survived Hitler had the physical or emotional ability to fulfill that commandment. But you do."

Chapter 33

Hamed once again agreed to help Ari travel incognito, though he felt disgruntled at being wakened in the middle of the night. Hamed's brother-in-law owned a taxi and, for the right price, would drive him through the West Bank, the place that Ari called Judea and Samaria. It was a route no longer safe for Israelis; therefore one the Mossad would not expect him to take.

Ari patted the money holder beneath his shirt. He felt like a rich man. "Don't spend it all in one place," Pincus had said when he gave it to him.

On the kibbutz he had received only a small allowance, the same as everyone else. The army had paid barely enough to buy cigarettes. Now he had more than sufficient funds to finance his search for Lily.

"Take off the beautiful suit," Hamed said without preamble. "Arab laborers don't wear silk suits." He fingered the smooth material of Ari's sleeve with his work-roughened fingers.

"Not my style anyway," Ari said as he undressed. He dropped the costly suit, bought recently in London, in a heap on the floor.

Hamed left the room and returned with a pair of gabardine trousers worn shiny in the seat, and a polyester shirt made in Pakistan.

Ari put the trousers on. "They're too tight."

Hamed nodded approvingly, "This is how my son dresses. Get rid of the fancy shoes, add a kaffiyeh, and you're a Palestinian."

"My Hebrew accent will give me away."

"You must not speak. My wife is preparing a fig poultice and a scarf to wrap around your neck. You have a bad throat infection, my friend."

Hamed said goodbye with no show of emotion, then shut the door. Ari heard the heavy metal bar fall into place as Hamed prepared to return to his bed.

Before stepping into the old Mercedes idling in the garden, Ari took time to look up. Stars like shattered glass sparkled overhead. It felt good to be back in the land. King David, the sweet psalmist of Israel, had watched his father's sheep, perhaps in this very spot. Ari felt a sense of anticipation at the thought of driving through the ancient territories of Judea and Samaria, something he had always wanted to do but couldn't as a modern Jew.

He checked his borrowed identity card. For tonight he was Hamed's elder son, Riad. At army checkpoints, Israeli soldiers would ask to see this card before they searched the Mercedes for explosives and weapons. Of course he couldn't talk because of his throat. He touched the soft wool scarf wrapped around his neck. Ari could hardly remember who he really was after playing so many roles in the last few months. One thing for certain, he would never again be the innocent kibbuztnik.

The engine purred as he settled into the soft cushions of the back seat. The driver, who didn't give his name, drove with a gentle foot on the gas pedal. They left Hamed's village and soon drove through the deserted streets of Bet Lehem.

Halfway between Bet Lehem and Jerusalem they approached the first army roadblock at the monument to the Matriarch Rachel. Israeli soldiers stood by the tomb of the mother who died giving birth to the last of Jacob's twelve sons. Rachel with her dying breath had called this infant *Ben-oni*, son of my sorrow. Jacob changed that to Ben-jamin, son of my right hand.

The driver stopped, rolled down the window and handed his papers to the soldier. Another soldier opened the back door and motioned for Ari to step out.

Ari barked a harsh cough that made the soldier step back a pace. "Put your identity card on the trunk," he ordered.

Within a few minutes they were again cruising down the road. In the distance, Ari saw the lights on the walls of the Old City. They turned east before they actually reached Jerusalem, passing through the villages of Abu Dis, Bethany, and then around the backside of the Mount of Olives.

The road zigzagged into the hills. In the frosty moonlight, the terraced grapevines appeared silvery blue. Ancient olive trees stood silhouetted in black against the moonlight.

Ari sat up straighter when he saw a road sign announcing the ancient ruins of Shiloh. He remembered Reza talking about the end of days or "until Shiloh comes." The Brotherhood thought he was the mysterious *Shiloh* who would gather the people and rule with a scepter. He had no idea what this meant in Muslim terms, or even Jewish, terms. He recalled from his history lessons in school that Shiloh had been the first home of the ark of the covenant.

He wished they could stop so that he could see the ancient site, but he knew it wouldn't be wise. Religious Jews had set up a caravan camp there in a futile attempt to hold on to sacred real estate, which in turn involved the Israeli Army, who had to guard them from terrorists.

Someday, I'll study the Torah and the Mishnah and find out what this all means, he vowed to himself. Ari's hand went up to his cheek, his palm covering the lion-shaped scar, as if he wanted to hide it.

As they approached the large town of Shechem, his driver spoke for the first time in hours. "I will not slow down. Neither of us is safe here."

"Why?"

"Hamas controls this town."

They passed by Joseph's tomb, then sped through Shechem's shuttered marketplace before continuing on past Mount Gerizim and out the other side of town near the slopes of Mount Ebal. In this very place Joshua Ben Nun had proclaimed: "Choose whom you will serve . . . as for me and my house, we will serve the Lord."

Whom do I serve? Ari asked himself. *The Brotherhood wants to pledge allegiance to me. Do I have any loyalty to my birth father's land? Do I serve Israel?*

Something nibbled at his memory as the car headed north. Something about Terah, the father of Abraham. He came from the land of the Chaldean or Mesopotamia. Ancient Persia. "Choose whom you will serve, whether the gods which your fathers served or the Lord."

It hit him with a force like thunder. *Abraham's father, like his, had also come from Persia.* Abram had left his father's people and set off on a journey, not knowing where he was going. Ari could relate to that. He thought of Reza and Ferideh, his only siblings. He knew he would never see them again. Where would his journey end? Like Abraham he hoped to end his days in Eretz Israel, the land of Israel.

In the back seat of the decrepit vehicle with the cracked leather seats, Ari had sudden clarity. He had done all he could for Pincus and the Mossad. His ties to Iran were irrevocably cut asunder.

"I will not serve the gods of my father, nor the secret service, nor the Brotherhood. I will serve the Lord Almighty," Ari said out loud in Hebrew.

Startled, the driver looked in his rear view mirror. Sweat trickled down the back of his neck. "Silence," he muttered in Arabic. "We must attract no attention."

Seeing fear in the driver's eyes, Ari stifled the urge to shout with joy. Despite the current danger, he felt inexpressibly peaceful. He would take Dr. Klein's good advice and marry Lily, but first he had to find her.

"How long before we get to the Galilee?" Ari asked.

""In twenty minutes we reach Dotan. My cousin lives there, and I need gas."

Dotan. Every village in the West Bank has a story, Ari thought. Here, the jealous brothers had thrown Joseph, the favorite son of Jacob, in a pit to die. Thinking of the young Joseph crying in the pit, he thought of his own beginnings in a garbage dumpster. Feelings of abandonment washed over him in waves that threatened to annul his newly found sense of joy and purpose.

But Joseph lived and rose to rule all of Egypt. His father and brothers eventually joined him in Egypt. This thought cheered Ari as they approached the outskirts of the Dotan.

Ari's driver woke his cousin, who was happy to see him, but not his passenger. He purchased a tank of gas and exchanged the blue West Bank plates for Israeli plates so that they could drive undetected in the Galilee.

At the driver's insistence, Ari shed his Arab clothing in exchange for something more Jewish. For one hundred shekels, the cousin sold him black trousers, a white dress shirt, and the skull cap worn by orthodox Jews.

They left Samaria as the sun crept over the mountains in Jordan, casting pink and gold tones over the landscape. On the right lay the road north to Rosh Pinna. Ari yearned to take the direct route but knew it would not be the safest choice. Instead, he asked the driver to take the left fork toward Nazareth. They circled around Mount Tabor, then climbed the foothills to Safed.

There he paid his driver from his dwindling stash of money. A blast of cold air blew through the streets, and he turned up his shirt collar and stuffed his fists into his pockets.

He stopped in front of a small cafe and looked through the streaked windows. After glancing both ways to check that he had no followers, he opened the cafe door and chose a stool at the counter. The aroma of strudel, fresh from the oven, hit his nostrils.

"Coffee, black," he said. "And some of whatever just came out of the oven."

The woman behind the counter set a steaming mug before him, along with apple strudel, then stood wiping the counter with a damp cloth.

"How do I get to Rosh Pinna from here?" he said, chewing his pastry.

"No buses today. Strike." She shrugged as if that was the end of the matter.

"Can I walk there?"

"Why not? It's not far." She raised her eyebrows for emphasis. "Go down the wadi, it's shorter than following the road."

Ari walked through the cobblestone streets until he came to the edge of town on the west side. A forest of young fir trees grew right up to the road. Following the downward slope of the land, he found the ravine and made good time downhill despite the boulders and rocks scattered on the landscape by recent flash floods.

He encountered no other hikers or picnickers due to the early hour. By ten a.m. he cautiously approached the back of an abandoned village. A three story-building with a fire escape dangling on one side stood strangely out of place. Not wanting to waste time, he continued on.

Five minutes later, fragrant olive wood smoke in the air told him he was near Rosh Pinna. Now to find the house of Rachel, he told himself.

Without knowing it, he chanced upon the same boy that Lily had encountered on her first day in Rosh Pinna. "Do you know where Rachel lives?" he inquired.

The boy nodded, then pointed to the right without missing a catch as the ball bounced back from the wall. "Nobody home."

"Thanks, I'll let myself in. I'm her cousin," Ari lied and immediately regretted it. Now he was committed to going in the front door. With the kid watching him, he casually strolled down the lane and stopped in front of Rachel's door. For show, he politely knocked once, then opened the door, calling out, "Rachel, it's me!"

The air in the house smelled of incense, dust, and stale cigarette smoke. It reminded him of his rented room in Bombay. He looked around for signs of Lily's presence but found not even a lingering whiff of her perfume. After checking each room, he waited on the balcony where he could escape into the wadi if necessary.

Chapter 34

Ari crumpled his last cigarette packet into a ball, narrowly missing a chattering squirrel with a sharp toss. He returned to pacing up and down the balcony.

Hearing the front door open, he stepped back in the shadows to observe but not be seen. A woman dressed like a Bedouin, in an ankle-length black tunic and a white head scarf, entered the house carrying a string shopping bag in each hand.

Dropping her bundles inside the door, she put her hand to the small of her back and muttered, "I'm too old to be shlepping groceries up hill."

Ari could detect an American accent in her Hebrew. Guessing that this must be Lily's hippie friend, he called out, "Ra-hel," pronouncing her name in the Hebrew manner.

She looked up, surprised, but showed no fear at finding a stranger on her balcony. People dropping in unannounced didn't appear to daunt her.

"Don't tell me," Rachel said. "Let me guess. Ari?"

He smiled, pleased that she knew enough about him to guess correctly. Lily must have described him. Nevertheless, he kept up the guessing game.

"How'd you know?"

"Certainly not by your black curls or bushy eyebrows. Lots of men have those features around here."

"Then how?" He thought his features were unique.

"The scar," Rachel replied.

Ari's hand stroked the small lion-shaped birthmark on his cheek. "Oh, this." He laughed trying to dismiss its importance. He felt uncomfortable talking about the mark that signified, at least to the Muslim Brotherhood, that he was the Mahdi. His eyes darted nervously around the room, then settled on her bundles.

"I'll help you bring in the food." He strode to her side and picked up the heavy bags.

If Rachel noticed his discomfort in talking about his birthmark, she didn't show it as he carried the foodstuff into the kitchen. After putting the milk and yogurt in the fridge and placing the fruit and vegetables in various baskets scattered on the counter, she asked the question he was waiting for.

"You want to know where Lily is? Right?"

"Yes."

"She *was* living here. Slept on the couch."

"And now?" Ari tried not to show his impatience but his curt tone must have given him away.

"She left us hippies for the messianics down the hill." Rachel's cynical tone revealed her attitude.

"How do I get there?"

Rachel laughed. "You sure don't waste time. Go rescue her from those guys."

"I never thought Lily would be drawn to the Black Hats."

"They aren't orthodox. They don't even wear a kippa."

"Then what?" Ari looked puzzled.

"Let's just say they celebrate Christmas."

"Goyim?"

"No, Jews. Or rather Christian Jews, or Jewish Christians, I don't know." Rachel put a tall, narrow pot on the burner to make

Turkish coffee. "You look as if you need something to drink."

"Thanks." Ari sank into a chair feeling as if all air had leaked out of him. It was getting complicated. He had never heard of Christian Jews. Neither had he considered what Lily might be going through during his absence. He'd expected her to be waiting for him. How foolish that had been. Her life would also have evolved, changing from day to day. He certainly couldn't expect her life to stop simply because he wasn't in it.

He watched Rachel as she let the coffee brew just to the boiling point, then withdrew the pot from the flames, letting the foam settle. She did this two more times, then poured the hot liquid into two small porcelain cups.

He took a gulp of the sweet coffee. "Ah," he said, "that's good."

"You want to talk about her?"

Ari nodded. He liked Rachel. Her handsome, open face made him trust her. If Lily had left this house, it must have been for a good reason. Rachel would have done her no harm.

"Did Lily talk to you about her conversations with angels?" He finished his coffee, wiping his mouth with the back of his hand and putting the cup back on its miniature saucer. This subject made him uncomfortable, but he tried not to show it.

"She did indeed. Things have been happening while you have been out of the country."

Ari narrowed his eyes, his mood turning dark. "Dr. Klein thinks Lily's delusional." He stared at Rachel to see her reaction.

"I don't think she's crazy, and neither do you." Rachel turned both their coffee cups upside down to let the grounds run down the sides. "After you disappeared at Ben Gurion," she pronounced each word distinctly and slowly to show her disapproval of his disappearing act, "Lily went back to Ain Karem.

Michael, the archangel, directed her in a dream to go to the Russian gardens."

The Russians again. How are they involved? Ari's thoughts spun ahead even as he listened to her words. He was now more sure than ever that the second man in the car that had nearly run over him was from the Muslim Brotherhood. The Russians? They supported radical groups on both sides of the political fence. Why not supply Tehran with modern technology and at the same time support a splinter group of Shi'ites banished to Damascus? The Russians were famous for playing both sides. If this was true, Lily was also in danger.

Rachel continued, "Lily found a stone stele in the convent gardens."

"A what?"

"A basalt monument with ancient writing carved on it."

"In what language?"

"Old Hebrew, what else?"

Ari shook his head in amazement. He thought nothing could catch him off guard again, but this information about Lily stunned him.

"Anyway," Rachel continued, "Lily took a tracing of it to the Rockefeller Museum for translation. Not long after that, this old lady, the mother superior, warned Lily to leave the village. That's when she came north to visit me." Rachel turned her tiny cup right side up and peered inside at the crusted coffee grounds.

Ari forced himself to put the subject of Russians, Shi'ites, and archangels aside temporarily. The words came out strained. "Do you think Lily wants to see me?"

Rachel picked up his coffee cup. "Let me read this." She peered into the tiny cup turning it toward the light. "You have serious opposition ahead of you, shown by the two mountains here." She pointed with her finger to two brown peaks. "I see a swift flowing river which indicates high energy. The rest is murky."

"You don't take this reading of the cups seriously?" Ari's eyebrows met together in an ominous angle.

"Yes and no. As to whether Lily wants to see you, she's in love with you, she said so."

Ari's lips turned up at the corners, his eyes shining with pleasure. His expressive eyebrows were now level. "How do I find her?"

"I'll take you there."

"Let's go."

Eli was in the underground prayer chamber and Dan was hoeing weeds in the garden when Rachel rang the bell. Lily opened the door and smiled tentatively when she saw Rachel standing on the front steps.

"I've missed you," Lily said sincerely.

Rachel laughed in her low throaty way. "You've missed someone more, I'll bet." She turned and called Ari's name.

As he stepped out from the shadow of the cyprus tree, Lily caught her breath and her eyes widened. "No, it can't be," she whispered. The man she had yearned to see for so long now stood before her. All she could focus on was the black skull cap perched precariously on his tousled hair.

"You've become a *baal chuvah*? A repentant Jew?" Tears of joy welled up then spilled over her lashes.

Ari took two long strides and enfolded her in a warm embrace. There was no need for words. Her tears and his hug sealed the reunion.

Lily raised her head, leaving a damp spot on his shoulder, and brought her lips up to meet his. They kissed long and hard as pleasant memories of their time together at Bet Shalom swept over her. A breeze swept down the hillside, stirring the branches of the cypress tree. A wind chime played spontaneous music in the background. She didn't want this moment to end.

Rachel stepped back, folded her arms, and chuckled indulgently as if she had been a paid matchmaker.

Then a shadow in the open front door announced the arrival of Eli. "Ahem," he coughed. "Do you want to come in?" He looked up and down the street to see if anybody was passing by.

While they sat under the stars hanging from the ceiling Eli excused himself to get his brother.

Ari sat close to Lily, as his trained eye took in the surroundings. He had chosen to sit with his back to a wall so no one could take him by surprise. Even the two tall windows barred with wrought iron made him nervous.

This living room was strange. He craned his neck to better see the swaying silver stars hanging from the ceiling. Then he read the intricately painted calligraphy on the wall. He recognized the words of the prophet Isaiah but couldn't place it in context to anything or anybody in this house. Eli had been in the room too short a time for Ari to get a fix on him.

Lily squeezed his hand and said, "You'll like the brothers, I know you will."

"The brothers? Is this some kind of monastery?"

Lily giggled from nervous excitement. "No, I mean they're really brothers, from the same mother and father."

The door opened and Ari stood, his posture defensive, but he sat down again when he saw that Daniel was carrying a wooden tray filled with a teapot, cups, and saucers. Months of living undercover had taken its toll on Ari's nerves. He used to know how to interact in a normal manner, but was this a normal situation? Better not let his guard down.

Daniel placed the tray on a low serving table, then introduced himself to Ari. His handshake was firm.

"Shall we speak in Hebrew or English?" Eli asked as he sat down next to his brother.

They all looked at Lily, who looked embarrassed. She smoothed the folds of her long skirt. "English is better for me."

Eli took charge of the conversation as Daniel poured the tea. He asked Ari where he was from and appeared surprised to hear that he'd been raised on nearby Kibbutz Shoshanat HaEmekim.

"Lily tells us you have been outside the country on a secret mission."

Ari coughed and looked at Lily. How much did she know? Who had told her? Fear made him suspect everyone.

"You don't have to tell us about your assignment. We understand about national security."

"Lily never mentioned anything about you being *haredi*, religious," Eli said staring at Ari's skull cap.

"Oh, this. Just another disguise." Ari took the cap off and stuffed it in his pocket.

"What are your plans now that you're back?" Rachel inquired with an innocent smile on her face.

Lily half turned so that she could see Ari's face. She continued to hold his hand. Rachel sat up a little straighter.

"Too soon to make any major decisions," he said, knowing he had already made the decision to marry Lily and leave Israel.

"Where are you staying tonight?" Eli asked.

Ari looked at Rachel, with one raised eyebrow.

"He's staying with me," Rachel replied.

Lily opened her mouth to say something, then closed it. She stared hard at Rachel.

Daniel looked at his brother, then back to Ari and Lily. Ever the peacemaker, he suggested that Ari could stay a few nights in the unused stable out back.

"There's a cot in the tack room. We'll give you a pillow and blanket."

Lily squeezed his hand so he knew that was what she wanted. He nodded to Daniel and said thanks.

He looked at Rachel and shrugged. The expression on her face revealed that this was really the way she had hoped the scenario would unfold.

Chapter 35

Ari and Lily's first day together in Rosh Pinna passed in quiet normalcy, as if there were no danger or urgency lurking in the shadows. Time stood still as they strolled through the fields behind the brothers' house, their feet crushing the fragrant sage and rosemary.

Reaching a rock outcropping overlooking the valley below, they sat and gazed at the fields of alfalfa that marked the boundaries of the nearest kibbutz. In the distance the Jordan River coiled like a silver snake, winding in and out between the scrub oak. In this pastoral Galilean setting, so unlike the harsh desert landscape of his recent experiences, Ari decided to tell Lily the truth. He felt compelled to tell her why his heart felt as cold and stiff as the corroded lava beds on the Golan.

"I'm the cause of so much death." He put his hand up to stop her protests. "My parents were murdered because of me." Trying to control the trembling in his voice he continued. "Dr. Rosen's death and the clinic's cook. Even the death of a British nurse because she befriended me in the orphanage."

Reading disbelief in Lily's horrified expression, he pulled out his wallet and handed her the snapshot taken on his first birthday by Miss Queller.

Lily reluctantly smiled when she saw the one fat candle on the chocolate cake. "That nurse must have loved you very much."

"What makes you say that?"

"A baby's first birthday picture treasured for all these years. She obviously didn't care that you're half Muslim and half Jew."

Ari shoved the snapshot back in his wallet as if he wanted to bury it. He gazed at a flock of cranes flying in formation over the valley. "Did you know these cranes come from Holland?" He didn't wait for a reply. "The Hula Valley is on their migratory path to North Africa. Must be getting cold in Europe."

"Why do you say you're responsible for those murders?" Lily asked, ignoring his diversionary talk of birds.

"The people who kidnapped me thought I was someone else. In their twisted version of things, everyone close to me had to die."

Too stunned to reply, Lily picked up his hand and held it against her cheek. He felt warm tears on his palm.

After revealing this much, he knew why he hesitated to tell Lily the truth. He felt conflicted about his brother Reza. He now knew Reza wasn't responsible for murdering his parents but he wasn't through with Abd Umar. How could he burden Lily with this?

Now she, too, gazed at the silver-gray cranes. With their slender necks stretched forward in graceful flight they looked like miniature planes. If she noticed Ari was holding something back, she said nothing.

Falling in love had been a new experience for Ari. Girls his age on the kibbutz had not appealed to him because he thought of them as sisters. Females in the army seldom occupied combat positions and did not train with the men, except for Gila.

He had briefly lusted for the female paratrooper who taught his unit how to jump. With her urging them on, no one hesitated to jump, no matter how scared.

It was different with Lily. He yearned to be transparent before her, to reveal his fears. Wanting and doing were two different things, though. When he imagined them together during the past few months it had seemed so easy. He would tell her everything, and her big, soft eyes would reveal unconditional acceptance.

Now, reunited at last, he feared she couldn't accept that he was half Iranian, his father a Shi'ite clergyman from the holy city of Qom. Yet, he had to get it out in the open. It weighed on his heart like one of the anchors dragging on a fishing boat in the Galilee.

"Lily, I need to tell you something." He traced his finger down the lifeline on the palm of her hand, then raised it to his lips and kissed her fingertips.

She smiled and closed her eyes.

"I always knew I was different from my companions on the kibbutz. It wasn't just that I was adopted." He gently let go of her hand to touch the birthmark on his cheek, then continued. "On my eighteenth birthday, my father told me that I was part Palestinian and part Jewish."

"Yes, I know that Ari. You told me in Bet Shalom when we first met. It makes no difference to me." She gazed at him with a longing that melted his heart. "But there's more, isn't there." She made it a statement, not a question.

"I've since learned more about my birth father."

"Just don't tell me he's Yasser Arafat," she said in a tone that implied she was not kidding.

Ari groaned.

"According to Jewish law, it doesn't matter who your father is. You're Jewish because of your mother," Lily said, then kissed him on the mouth.

He returned her kiss with equal fervor, feeling the pulse beating in the hollow of her neck like a trapped butterfly.

"Don't stop," Lily said at last.

Ari's blood raced through his veins. He wanted to continue holding her in his arms until the sun set and the first evening star came out to bless them. It was as if all nature conspired to bring them together. Honesty compelled him to remove his arms from around her waist.

"My father isn't a Palestinian."

He noticed Lily's face flush with confusion.

"I'm part Iranian. Son of a Shi'ite mullah."

Lily looked relieved, yet still confused.

"According to Muslim law, it is the father who counts. It doesn't matter who your mother is," Ari explained.

The perplexity in her expression caused Ari to put off telling her more about the tekiyah in Damascus, the Muslim Brotherhood, and his so-called messiahship as the Mahdi. For now, they would be safe in Rosh Pinna. Nobody knew their whereabouts, not Reza and the Brotherhood, nor the Russians, not even the Mossad.

He took Lily in his arms again and held her tight against his chest as he murmured fragments of the ninety-first psalm. He could only hope that his love would shield her from the pestilence that lurks in darkness and the destruction that wastes at noonday.

Chapter 36

One afternoon, without preamble, Eli began to speak about *set times* and something called the *end of days*.

Ari shuddered as if snow from the nearby Hermon had drifted down on him. He could hardly breathe under the weight as he remembered the opulent tekiyah in Damascus and the cold but polite Abd Umar in his green turban. What had the mystic holy man said to him? Something about a star rising out of Jacob in the end of days.

Then a wild surge of hope melted the ice on his chest. Maybe Eli and Daniel could help him sort out this business of the Mahdi.

"I can't tell you all the details," he began hesitantly, "but I was in Damascus recently." He looked for skepticism in their eyes and finding none, continued. "I met a Shi'ite holy man who related a prophecy about the Star of Jacob in connection with the end times."

The atmosphere in the sitting room changed from friendly warmth to electric urgency. Eli and Daniel, slouching against a pile of throw pillows, sat up straight, their feet now firmly on the floor.

"Say that again," Eli said in a soft voice that betrayed the iron will behind his genial personality.

Ari could feel prickles on the back of his neck. What had he said that alarmed them? Damascus? No Israeli had ever gone to Syria and come back alive. Did they think he was lying? Or was it the mention of the holy man? Or the Star of Jacob?

The tension in the room filled the air like static electricity. In the background Ari could hear Lily puttering in the kitchen, and he willed her to stay there.

"What kind of holy man? Syrian?" Daniel said, his voice breaking the silence in a hoarse whisper.

Ari thought he could trust them, but why were they now on high alert? Should he tell them about the Mahdi? Would they understand? The Mossad had exploited this information for its own purposes.

But these two brothers living in this rustic house in a small village were not like Pincus or his agency. In a surge of good faith, Ari decided to tell them the truth, at least as much as he knew of it.

"Persian. The man was from Iran. Exiled to Damascus."

Daniel's eyebrows went up as he glanced at his brother. Eli nodded in reply to the unspoken question.

"We aren't trying to pry but we have reason to believe that a significant threat is coming to Israel from Iran. Do you want to hear more?" Eli asked.

Ari couldn't believe he'd heard correctly. How could they know about Iran's nuclear weapons program? Only he and the Mossad had this information. He wiped his sweating palms on his knees, craving a cigarette, mentally kicking himself for leaving them in the tack room. He answered Eli with a simple "Yes."

Eli picked up a well worn copy of the Hebrew Scriptures. "You no doubt recall the story of Balak and Balaam."

Ari nodded, though he couldn't remember the actual story.

"Balak, prince of Moab, commissioned Balaam, the wise man from the East, to curse Israel and turn them back to Egypt. Instead, Balaam went into a trance and blessed the tribes of

Israel. "How goodly are thy tents, O Jacob and thy tabernacles, O Israel," he read from the Hebrew Scriptures.

Ari listened intently, but wondered what all this had to do with Iran. His puzzlement showed on his face.

"Patience, my friend," Daniel said, continuing, "Three times Balak asked the seer to curse the Israelites and three times he blessed them. Finally, Balaam uttered a prophecy about what would happen in the latter days."

> *There shall come a star out of Jacob,*
> *and a scepter shall rise out of Israel.*
> *Out of Jacob shall come he that*
> *shall have dominion.*

"I still don't see the connection to Iran," Ari said. "Or to me," he added.

"My brother and I have studied this subject for years. We've found many references to ancient manuscripts that speak of the Star of Jacob."

Ari wanted to hear more. Why would Reza and his people believe in a messiah that came out of Israel? Why would the Muslim world follow such a man?

Like a well rehearsed duo, Eli and Daniel spoke with fervor.

"This Balaam is thought to be the precursor to Zoroaster," said Daniel.

"He founded this religion in Persia, before Islam." Eli added.

"Yes, and it is believed by some that Balaam taught Zoroaster about the principles of light and darkness warring for dominion over the earth," continued Daniel.

"Balaam was the first wise man, or magi, from the East. Zoroastrians then spread their message across Mesopotamia as far as Damascus. Islam picked it up, and there are even Jewish references to the star of Jacob in Essene scrolls found near the Dead Sea."

As the brothers continued to expound on their theory of what the Star of Jacob implied, Lily appeared in the doorway. Only Ari saw her. With his eyes, he motioned for her to leave, but she folded her arms across her chest and stood in place.

His mind followed what the brothers were saying. At the same time, he weighed the consequences of Lily's finding out about his status as the Shi'ite messiah.

"It's thought that the magi or wise men, who were reported to have followed the star to Bet Lehem after the birth of Jesus, are descendants of Balaam. Iranian holy men, or magicians as they were known then."

Ari took a deep breath and motioned for Lily to come and sit next to him. She smiled at the brothers, then crossed the room and sat by Ari's side.

"So, you think there is a connection between my encountering a Persian magi in Damascus and this prophecy about a ruler coming out of Jacob? You might be right. Abd Umar thinks I am the fulfillment of this prophecy. He calls me the Mahdi, or Hidden One. I will restore peace on earth." He laughed without mirth, feeling more bitter than ironic.

Lily coughed in a dry, tight way that revealed her uneasiness. He felt her body stiffen even as she leaned closer to him.

"We see a connection, but we're not jumping to any conclusions about you personally," Eli replied. He looked at his brother for affirmation.

"It's uncanny that you should come in just now," Daniel said looking at Lily. "We also find your story most unusual."

Ari felt puzzled, but put his arm around Lily. How could her delusions about the archangel Michael have anything to do with this?

As if he could read Ari's thoughts, Eli spoke first. "Lily has found a stone marker that might be from the tomb of King David. It has references to the restoration of the fallen tabernacle of David."

His brother continued for him. "Whether you believe in angels or not, she did find a significant artifact. Furthermore, an archaeologist from the Rockefeller Museum said it mentions the end times."

Ari glanced at Lily. Their meeting at Bet Shalom had been no accident. He gave her hand a squeeze. Still, it all seemed so preposterous. Why was this happening to them? His head felt as if someone were holding it under water. He wanted to come up for air, take Lily, and run for the hills. Instead, he looked down at the rough, hand-hewn stones that made up the floor. A stone mason had patiently chiseled out each piece and made them fit together in precision with the others. It was craftsmanship that bordered on art, with a rustic beauty that could not be diminished by his rough-soled boots sitting on it.

He continued to muse on this theme. Maybe he and Lily were pieces in a divine plan. Chiseled and placed so they fit together without the need of mortar. What about the brothers? Or Rachel, Dr. Klein, Reza? Were they also part of the pattern? "I don't know," he muttered over and over in quiet anguish and wonder.

Daylight faded from the windows as the twilight deepened in Rosh Pinna. They were sitting in shadows, each with his own thoughts.

Then Eli stood and turned on a table lamp. "I think we've spoken enough for now. Let's go eat whatever Lily has been preparing most of the afternoon."

They spent the evening sitting around the kitchen table, eating bowls of vegetable soup accompanied by hunks of bread slathered in butter. Lily had even baked a chocolate cake using an aluminum pan placed over the gas ring.

"Not bad," Ari said as he stuffed a piece of cake in his mouth, then washed it down with hot coffee.

"Your turn to cook tomorrow," Lily challenged Ari.

"*Ain bayoit*, no problem. Don't you know that everybody does kitchen duty on a kibbutz? I've known my way around a kitchen since I was ten." He glanced at the two-ring gas burner sitting on the counter. "And at my kibbutz, we have real stoves and real ovens."

They all laughed in response. The hot soup, cake, and coffee had restored their high spirits. All talk of mystics and magi had ceased, at least for the evening.

Ari allowed himself to relax and enjoy this time together with Lily. He only wished that, when the evening was over, and they all went to their beds, that Lily could join him out in the tack room. He could tell by the high color in her cheeks and the loving glances she kept giving him that she felt the same. His portion of happiness had never been so great.

He should have known that it couldn't last. A loud knocking on the back door wakened every nerve in his body.

"Don't open it until Lily and I are gone." He grabbed Lily's hand, pulled her away from the table and headed for the front door. The loud banging continued.

"Hey, I know you're in there! It's me. Rachel."

Eli opened the door and invited her in. Ari and Lily stopped at the front door and stared back at Rachel's disheveled appearance.

"Give me a drink of water," she said. "I ran all the way here." She drank the water in swift gulps. As she waited for her breathing to return to normal, she motioned for them to sit and listen.

"Someone is making inquiries around the village about Ari.

He's also asking about an American woman with curly hair. He's offering a reward."

Lily fingered her shoulder length curls. "Did this stranger by any chance have a Russian accent?"

"Yes." Rachel looked at Lily with pity in her eyes. "KGB thug, if you ask me."

"No one is taking his money I hope," said Daniel.

"Of course not. However, they're staying the night at the Rosh Pinna Guest House.

"How do you know that?" Ari asked.

"His Mercedes is parked in front."

Ari felt sure the Muslim Brotherhood was working with the Russians from Ain Karem. Somehow they had traced him to Rosh Pinna. Maybe the taxi driver's cousin in Dotam had given him away. He knew that Reza's group would not harm him, but Lily was in jeopardy. The Mahdi did not have a consort. They would eliminate her as ruthlessly as they had the others.

"How do we get out of Rosh Pinna unseen?" Ari looked to Eli.

Eli's countenance showed resolve and calm courage. He thought a moment, then spoke with quiet authority. "You can leave here through the back fields. Keep walking until you get to the ruins of Hatzor. It will take maybe two hours in the dark. Stay there until sunrise. By then, my brother and I will have devised a way to pick you up."

Chapter 37

They each hastily packed a shoulder bag with a change of clothing and their passports. Ari possessed an Israeli passport in his name and a fake Cypriot passport in the name of Yusef Ben Haddad. Lily carried her American passport.

Farewells were brief and to the point. Rachel kissed Lily on both cheeks, then embraced Ari. "Next year in Yerushalim," she sniffed, trying to hold back the tears that told she knew such a reunion was unlikely.

The brothers pronounced the Aaronic blessing: "The Lord bless thee, the Lord keep thee, the Lord make his face to shine upon thee."

Together they all walked through the courtyard and around the barn. Near the vegetable garden, where radishes and leeks glimmered in the moonlight, they waved goodbye for the last time. Unspoken, but keenly felt, was the knowledge that this configuration of friends would never be together again.

Hand in hand, Ari and Lily trekked determinedly across the uncultivated fields. The night sky blazed with a myriad of stars as if a celestial presence guided their footsteps north.

Within a very short time they approached the outskirts of the modern settlement town named after the ancient city of Hatzor. A mongoose, slinking to capture a hen from a farmer's chicken house, heard their footsteps and made a hasty retreat into the sage bushes. The smell of crushed sage wafted up to their noses.

They kept well away from the modest houses because civilian guards would be walking the streets in constant vigil against terrorism.

Once again Ari was running for his life, crossing unfamiliar terrain in the moonlight. Only this time he felt heartened to have Lily by his side. He squeezed her hand to let her know how much he loved her. Fate had irrevocably linked their lives.

Skirting the town, they slowly made their way towards the excavated ruins of Hatzor. If all went well, Eli and Dan would meet them there at sunrise. "God willing," Ari whispered under his breath.

As they made their way across the deserted fields, Ari recalled that he had visited the ancient site of Hatzor years ago on a kibbutz field trip. Now he regretted not paying more attention to the guide who had led his group through the ruins. He did remember that thousands of years ago, Hatzor sat at the crossroads of two international trade routes and therefore was the head of all the northern kingdoms of the Canaanites. Joshua destroyed the place, but Solomon rebuilt it.

Ari also remembered the explanation of how the archaeologist, Professor Yigael Yadin, had located the exact spot to excavate the citadel. Yadin had simply asked the local farmers why they preferred to have their late afternoon lunch break on a certain hilltop. The farmers replied that on this particular spot a cool breeze came every afternoon to relieve the afternoon heat. Yadin's men dug right there and, to every one's surprise but Yadin's, uncovered the citadel.

What good these recollections would do him now, Ari didn't know. He just had to get them safely there and wait for Daniel and Eli to show up. He hoped that the brothers had a safe haven to take them to after that. He had to trust them. There was no other choice.

It took no more than two hours to make the distance from Rosh Pinna to the ruins of Hatzor. In the moonlit night, the Tel revealed a pale yet rugged beauty not appreciated in the harsh light of the sun. Marble pillars, thick as cedars of Lebanon, stood guard over the deserted palace.

"We need to find a place to hide." Ari spoke in a soft but urgent tone. "Walk behind me following my footsteps." They began the ascent of the beaten earth ramparts that led up one hundred and twenty feet to the citadel area.

"This was once a big mound. It took hundreds of workmen and years of labor to uncover these ramparts." Ari spoke in hushed tones, but there was no need for silence. The only presence besides theirs was an owl hunting for field mice.

Beside a magnificent palace gate, they found a remnant of a room, with low walls and no roof. Ari unpacked a lightweight army-issue tarp from his backpack and spread it on the powdery earth floor. Lily sat down beside him to catch her breath. Ari handed her a canteen.

Lily took a long drink and lay back to look up at the night sky. "I always knew I was destined for a palace." A wistful smile crossed her lips.

Ari lay on his back next to her and sighed with relief and wonder. The constellations appeared close enough to reach out and touch. The stars blinked as if in some cosmic message they could decipher.

Lily turned on her side and gazed at Ari. "I nearly gave up waiting for you to come back."

His longings and fears melted away as he put his arms around her. In the shadow of a splendid marble gate, built by one of Solomon's architects, he held her close for a moment.

Then he sat up and took her hand in his. "Lily, will you marry me?"

Straight away she got to her feet and pulled him up as well. "Yes, yes, yes."

Ari smiled and looked up at the stars. "At least your answer is not ambiguous."

"Let God and all the angels bear witness, Ari and Lily belong to each other," She shouted into the night. Just then two shooting stars blazed across their field of vision.

"Come, sit beside me, my love, and we'll watch for the dawn."

The sky slowly changed from velvet black to pale gray tinged with pink as the sun rose over the Golan Heights. The night dew sparkled in their hair like jewels.

"Dan and Eli will be here soon. We have to be ready to move quickly." Ari then scrambled up a rampart to survey the road below. No vehicles traveled the access road from the main highway to the site. He scanned the nearby kibbutz for signs of movement and saw only a few individuals, small as stick figures from this distance and height. He guessed they were heading for the dining room. He turned and looked north as the first sun rays struck the highest peak of Mount Hermon.

He knew Damascus was only an hour drive across the Golan. He mentally pictured Abd Umar in his white robes and the green headdress of the Seyyed. Ari, too, was a Seyyed, a direct descendant of Mohammed. Ari shuddered, and not just from the early morning chill.

Lily stretched her stiff limbs and climbed the rampart after Ari. "How do you think the brothers will get a vehicle?"

"I don't know, but we will see them approach from the main road." He was worried, but he didn't share his unease with Lily.

As daybreak turned to a hot morning, Ari grew more and more agitated as they waited for the brothers to come. "We can't stay here much longer. Tour groups will start showing up soon." Troubled, he glanced at his watch.

"What could be keeping them?" Lily asked.

He saw the fear in her eyes and knew he would have to make different plans for their escape. His mind had already pictured Daniel and Eli murdered in their beds, like Dr. Rosen, sacrificial lambs on the altar of some mad deity. He glanced one last time at his watch.

"We're not waiting." Ari spoke in firm determination.

Lily tried to voice her concern, but Ari gently cut her off. "Trust me."

Ari packed the tarp in his bag, then picked up handfuls of loose dirt and pebbles to scatter over the spot. "Help me cover our tracks."

The first tour bus of the morning pulled into the parking area at the foot of the mound. Tourists wearing sun hats and shorts hiked exuberantly up the path, led by a veteran Israeli tour guide. "Professor Yigael Yadin first excavated this site in 1955." His voice carried over the site as Ari and Lily slipped away into the foothills.

Ari knew the town of Merom lay approximately four miles northeast of Hatzor. From there he figured they could catch a bus to the port city of Haifa. As they hiked up the ravine, he formulated plans to steal a sailboat in the harbor, then sail to Cyprus. He already had a Cypriot passport. He had no idea where they would eventually settle. *One step at a time*, he murmured under his breath.

"What did you say?" Lily asked.

"I have a plan, my love. You and I will sail away to another land, another place."

"Do we have to leave Israel? What about the stone I found in the garden?" She stopped to catch her breath and reached for the canteen on Ari's belt.

Chapter 38

Daniel and Eli returned in silence to the hidden chapel in their basement. Eli struck a match and lit a thick candle before sitting on one of the small stools. His brother knelt on the camel-hair rug, knowing from experience that the scratchy fibers would help keep him awake during a long vigil.

As was their custom, they waited in silence before the Lord. They never made direct petitions to the Almighty, or tried to sway the outcome of this or that event. They listened for the *still small voice*. As they settled down for a long night of intercession, they knew they must quell the vivid image of Ari and Lily fleeing through the countryside.

In the deepest part of the night, when every soul in Rosh Pinna was asleep, even the neighbors' annoying dog, they heard the faint sound of footsteps above their heads. They felt rather than heard the vibrations of boots plodding across the stone floor. The brothers' grandparents had also hidden in a cellar, ears straining to hear the shuffle of booted men above their heads. Like a mantra, their mother had repeated the story to them all through their childhood, always finishing with the words, "Never again." But it was happening again, and in their own homeland.

Dan and Eli held hands and continued praying, their lips moving silently. If they must die, it would be united. Unlike their grandparents who had prayed "Hear O' Israel, the Lord thy God is one," Eli and Daniel prayed for the enemies of God to be scattered. In some mysterious way, they felt Ari and Lily had been entrusted with the future of Israel. This couple must escape from the malevolent men stalking them in the rooms above.

They heard muffled sounds of furniture being violently kicked over. Then the kitchen door opened. They heard steps crossing the courtyard and a commotion in the tack room where Ari had slept. The intruders returned to the courtyard. They were only ten feet away from the two hiding in the basement.

Daniel's knees trembled violently. His brother put his hand across his knees to steady him. They held their breath, waiting for the assassins to discover the door to the basement.

Muffled voices in some unknown language began what sounded like curses or imprecations. It wasn't Arabic, possibly Persian. Abruptly the voices stopped. Daniel and Eli shut their eyes. Total silence reigned for fifteen long seconds. Then it was over. The intruders left the courtyard, returning to their parked car.

Badly shaken, Eli and Daniel came out of the prayer chamber convinced that it was too risky to take a vehicle to Hatzor to pick up Ari and Lily. The two would have to make it alone, *B'esrat ha'Shem*, with the help of the Lord.

The fleeing couple made it to the port of Haifa without detection, but Ari had second thoughts about sailing a stolen boat to Cyprus. He consoled himself with the thought that no kibbutznik knew how to sail. He was a farmer, not a sailor. Instead he bought a ticket for the next ship leaving for Larnaca, the port city of Cyprus, traveling under the assumed identity given to him by the Mossad, Yusef Ben Haddad.

Lily bought her ticket separately, traveling on her American passport as Lily Towzer of Far Rockaway, New York. They boarded the vessel at noon and stayed in their separate cabins.

At the edge of dawn and still unable to sleep, Lily tapped on Ari's cabin door. He rolled out of the bunk, slightly nauseous from the motion of the waves. Using the peephole to see into the corridor, he smiled when he saw Lily. He opened the door and cautiously looked up and down the corridor before pulling her inside.

She made herself comfortable at the foot end of his bunk. "So, you can't sleep either?"

"No, I'm still tense. Talk to me about your childhood. Maybe, that will help me unwind."

"Why don't you tell me about the children's house on your kibbutz?" Lily, like most Americans, found it curious that children on the kibbutz lived in separate houses from their parents. The idea fascinated and repelled her at the same time.

He obliged her by recalling what it was like to sleep with the sounds of the breathing and gentle sighs of five children in nearby cots. It gave him comfort to talk about those happy times.

Without warning, though, his thoughts turned to Reza and Ferideh. How were they raised? Did their father and mother put them to bed or did servants?

Still thinking about his half brother and sister, he self-consciously touched the scar on his cheek. "This is their proof that I am their messiah." He didn't try to hide his bitterness at being the recipient of their misguided adoration.

"You mean the Muslim Brotherhood?" Lily asked. "Or your brother and sister?"

This wasn't where she wanted the conversation to go in the pale light of the new morning. She didn't want to deal with his status as the so-called Holy One.

"Where do I fit in this picture? Does their messiah have a bride?" She tried to sound lighthearted, but her voice failed her.

Ari kissed her, as much to reassure himself as her. "Ha! I can have as many concubines as I wish." Ari tried to lighten the mood.

"Says who?"

"Reza," he replied.

Lily sat in the narrow bunk, leaning against the wall. "Remember what I told you about the archangel Michael?"

Ari detected a new edge in her voice and leaned toward her. "Go on, I'm listening."

"What if it's divine providence that brought us together at Bet Shalom?"

"I can accept that," Ari cautiously replied.

"The angel told me in a dream how to find the stele in the Russian garden. Its inscription says something about the end times. What if these are the end times?"

"Nuclear bombs falling on Tel Aviv and Jerusalem would certainly be the end for the Jews. You know, the Samson Option. Is that what you mean?"

"I don't know what I mean. But it might fit together. You going undercover to Iran. Returning as a modern day prophet. Meanwhile, I find what is, according to the professor at the museum, the lost burial place of King David."

Now Ari caught Lily's excitement. "Yes, Daniel and Eli talked about the restoration of the fallen tabernacle of David in the end times."

"Perhaps the miracle that Israel needs has something to do with what lies buried beside David's bones."

"The ark of the covenant?"

"Why not?"

"No, Eli was emphatic on that point," Lily replied. "We can't let Hollywood movies influence us. According to him, the ark is already in the heavens."

"Should we go back and excavate the burial tomb ourselves?" The thought energized Ari and he would have turned back at that moment if Lily's life was not in danger.

"We have to continue on to Cyprus and see what happens. Michael will guide us, I know he will." Lily squared her shoulders with a determination that made Ari love her all the more.

But as she thought about the heart-racing energy she had felt pulsing from the earth in the garden of the Russian convent, Lily knew she would go back one day.

By mid-morning, their ship reached the busy harbor at Larnaca, where they disembarked separately and, as they had arranged, met at the bus station. They traveled inland to the capital city nestled in the foothills. Nicosia was a divided city, one half held by Greeks and the other by Turks. This situation felt natural to Ari, who had never known a state of peaceful existence since his unwanted birth during the Six Day War, when Israel's neighbors attacked on three fronts.

While they ate lunch in Nicosia, a man sat down uninvited at their patio table. He quietly identified himself as a friend of Motti Pincus. It didn't surprise Ari to learn the Mossad had followed them. He hoped the Brotherhood had not been as successful.

The agent helped himself to a piece of warm pita bread and told them it wasn't safe for them to stay in Nicosia. He had already arranged for them to cross the border to the Turkish side. He handed them each a new passport.

Lily opened her passport then immediately asked to see Ari's. "We're man and wife!" she gleefully exclaimed.

"Safest way to travel," the agent replied dryly.

Ari held the man's gaze. "We're planning to get married, anyway."

"Wait a minute. This isn't official and I'm not going any further until it is." Lily primly straightened her skirt and crossed her ankles.

The agent looked quizzically at Ari, as if to say, it's your call.

Ari stood up, taking Lily's hand. "Let's go to a civil judge and do it."

"What about a rabbi and the huppa?" Lily said, now unsure.

Taking charge of the rapidly changing situation, the Mossad agent reassured Lily that she could have a religious ceremony in the future. Now, she would have to settle for a quick civil ceremony that he would arrange in front of a local magistrate.

Lily reluctantly agreed, but insisted she would have to buy a dress before the ceremony. The agent hurried off to make arrangements.

Lily and Ari hurried down the street looking in shop windows. They stopped in front of a boutique that sold women's clothing. Lily tried on a sleeveless, white sheath that came to her knees. She picked a large, straw sun-hat to go with the outfit, insisted that she needed new sandals.

Ari looked anxiously at his watch. "Shoes will have to wait for another time, my darling." He hurriedly picked out a new white shirt. "No, I don't need a tie," he told the insistent shopkeeper.

They went to the seedy town hall, where an official in a tight-fitting black suit sat behind a desk. The overhead fan barely stirred the papers on his desk. He half stood, then sat down again, wiping his sweating face with a clean handkerchief.

Ari appeared nervous, fidgeting with the stiff collar on his new shirt. He unbuttoned the two top buttons.

Lily's long, deeply tanned legs contrasted nicely with the white linen dress. She wore the straw hat at a rakish angle. But this was not the wedding ceremony she had dreamed of.

At the last minute, the Mossad agent refused to be the required witness. He mumbled something about keeping his cover.

The flustered magistrate left the room and came back with a female clerk. She alone smiled during the brief ceremony and even wept a tear or two when Ari placed the turquoise and diamond ring on Lily's finger. Ari would someday tell Lily how he had protected this ring through water and fire in the Persian Gulf. Now it was enough to see the glow of love in her eyes. When it was over, the bride and groom rushed off to the Turkish side of the island, where a hired fishing boat waited to take them to Rhodes.

They spent a week of quiet bliss at the Pension Tehran, in the old city. The Mossad agent had recommended it as a safe haven. The Greek owner of the pension told them he had lived thirty years in the capital of Iran and still had fond memories of his first home.

Another displaced soul, Ari thought wryly. How does the Mossad find them?

As newlyweds, they seldom left their room. The proprietor, happy to oblige the bride and groom, discreetly arranged room service. After the couple moved on to Athens, two Mossad agents showed up and cut the page out of his guest book that listed Ari and Lily's new names. He obliged them, because he liked the young couple, and not just the five-hundred-dollar bribe.

With their new identities, cash, credit cards, and even a checkbook, generously provided by Motti Pincus, they completed a convoluted itinerary through Athens, London, New York, Chicago, and they finally arrived in Phoenix, Arizona. Pincus even hired a taxi driver, a tight-lipped ex-New Yorker, who met them at Sky Harbor.

The outside temperature of one hundred and fifteen degrees reminded Ari of the desert between Tehran and Qom. Yet, he felt a chill on the back of his neck despite the heat. He would always feel the need to look over his shoulder, or scan the faces of passing strangers. Lily sensed his discomfort and turned to him with raised eyebrows. He reassured her by taking her hand as they drove in silence from Phoenix to Tucson.

Lily looked with approval at the white-walled, red-roofed villas silhouetted against the purple mountains. She could get used to a garden of saguaros, she told herself. But the driver continued on the Interstate Eight until they were on the other side of Tucson.

Ari read a highway sign that said they were not far from Tombstone. "Wyatt Earp? For real?" He couldn't believe his eyes.

The driver looked at him through the rearview mirror and shrugged. "You want I should make a detour there?"

"No, continue as planned," Ari replied. He had no idea where they were going. Pincus had deliberately not given him details of their final destination. If he were recaptured by the Muslim Brotherhood, he would not be able to reveal anything.

The driver turned off on a secondary road that wound between rolling brown hills. They continued due south for forty-five minutes without seeing a single town or habitation.

The newlyweds settled in Patagonia, Arizona, a hauntingly beautiful, if desolate area of cattle ranches and vineyards. It was also near the Mexican border. A strategic location, not lost on Ari, who liked the idea of a back-door escape route.

Lily is certain the archangel will know where to find her. Ari fervently hopes Reza will never find him.

An Excerpt from
The Time of Jacob's Trouble
by Sharon Geyer
Coming soon from FaithWalk Publishing
www.faithwalkpub.com

Chapter 1

Today was different from all other days because a letter postmarked Jerusalem came in the mail. Lily handled it as if it were hot to the touch. She placed it face down on the kitchen table to await Ari's return from the vineyards. Then she sat at the kitchen table staring at the letter as she drank glass after glass of lemonade, trying to put out the flames within her.

The local mailcarrier, a sturdy Apache woman born and raised on the reservation in the White Mountains, never put more than advertising circulars and utility bills in their mailbox. Except today.

The sun set in the west, casting long shadows on the lone saguaro cactus. Through the window Lily watched Ari pull into the gravel driveway and park beside the house. Lily stood and turned on the kitchen light just as he walked in the back door.

"Want a cold drink?" she said after kissing him harder and longer than usual.

Ari held her at arm's length and smiled. "What's new?" Their ardor had never cooled, but Lily was usually busy cooking dinner at this time of day. Ari's nose told him that nothing was boiling or frying on the stove, so he continued to gaze at Lily.

Her eyes went involuntarily to the table top.

"It's from Jerusalem. No return address."

Ari stared at the white envelope as if it were a rattlesnake on his dinner table. Beads of perspiration dampened his upper lip and armpits. "I'll have that drink." he said, and sat on a wooden chair close to the letter.

Lily went to the refrigerator, grateful to have something to distract her from the business at hand. She popped the top of the cold bottle of Mexican beer and handed it to her husband.

"No need to panic." He wiped the foam off his upper lip before picking up the letter. "It's addressed to me." He held it up to the light, then ran his fingers over the envelope. Lily knew he was searching for the feel of some object that should not be in a letter. Finding nothing, he pulled out his pocket knife and slit one side open. A single sheet of paper slid out and lay on the table. He picked it up and read, "The time has come for the Hidden One to make himself known and fill the world with justice."

Ari's face paled under his dark tan. He stroked the lion-shaped scar on his left cheek as he looked with anguish at Lily. "They know where we are."

The magnitude of the threat lay beyond the threshold of Lily's conscious thought. She tried to remain rational and calm, though she had always known that this day would come. She had made Arizona her home. She cultivated her desert garden and secretly hoped to raise a child here. She glanced at the Mexican tile floors, the hand-woven carpets she had so carefully chosen, the blue-and-white crockery in the white cupboard.

On the map, Patagonia lies southwest of Tombstone, not many miles from the Mexican border. Here, Lily had enjoyed the routine of life hidden from the malevolent flow of events in the Middle East.

In front of their rented adobe house, Lily had planted a cactus garden, dominated by a three-armed saguaro. Behind the house grew a tenacious acacia tree that had spread its roots deep and wide to suck moisture from the dry soil. The wind intermittently blew through the faded rag strips tied to its narrow but supple branches.

The acacia tree was Lily's monument to Dr. Rosen's memory. Whether the Native Americans of the Southwest influenced her, or the Bedouin of the Negev, she couldn't say. It was true that the first acacia tree she ever saw had been on a trip to Elat.

Passing through the Negev, the only color was the multicolored rags tied to the occasional wind-bent tree. She never learned why the Bedouin did this, but she guessed that the women of the tribe did this to mark a special passage in their lives. From a distance the different colored strips of cloth looked like brightly colored parrots. Lily thought they were poems of joy for the birth of a healthy infant, or prayers of grief to ease the pain of disappointment or loss.

Lily knew a lot about disappointment. The months had turned into years, and she and Ari finally quit thinking about having a child. Ari felt secretly relieved. Abandoned at birth, his feelings about being a parent were different from Lily's. His family tree had whole branches missing. What facts he did know about his father scared him more than knowing nothing.

The acacia tree behind their house was a living monument in honor of a man murdered in the prime of life. Unspoken, but always present, was their decision to name their first born after Samuel Rosen. In reality, the strips of cloth were in memory of both Samuels, the murdered one and the one who would never be born.

Ari's earlier experience tending roses in the Galilee stood him in good stead when he applied for work in the local vineyards that grew on the gentle hills surrounding Patagonia. He enjoyed rising before dawn, greeting the first rays of light as he drove out to the fields to prune the vines. He had no need of lifting weights in a gym, even had such facilities been available in Patagonia, which they were not. The one-street town had a courthouse, two saloons, one cafe, a library, and one gas station.

Ari looked much like the Mexican grape pickers who showed up when the fruit was ripe, then disappeared when the harvest was over. He was medium in height with dark curly hair and dark eyes. People in town couldn't place his accent, but they knew it wasn't local. The owner of the vineyard, himself a transplant from another culture, time, and place, didn't care where Ari was from. It was enough that he worked hard, was never sick, and never asked for a raise.

On the other hand, Lily spoke with a New York accent that sounded comical to the southwest farmers and ranchers who came into Patagonia to buy groceries or have a beer. She mostly kept to herself, avoiding the searing sun during the heat of the day. Lily did patronize the small library adjacent to the courthouse, reading autobiographies or history books. Ari occasionally took his fifteen-year-old jeep to the repair shop attached to the one gas station in town. The mechanic told his wife that he thought Art, as the locals called him, was from Bosnia, or somewhere like that.

Now the letter from Jerusalem had changed everything.

"I'll pack our bags," Lily said, fiercely determined to remain pragmatic in the face of a crisis. "Do we need to contact Pincus before we leave?"

"The Mossad?" Ari growled the name of the Israeli intelligence service. "There's a traitor there. How else could the Muslim Brotherhood have found us?"